HUNTER JONES JOINS THE CIVIL WAR

(Arkansas)

Jinx (Julian) Olson

Village Creek Publishing LLC

ISBN-9781451511741

Cover design by: Julian Olson
Library of Congress Control Number: 2018675309
Printed in the United States of America

*Dedicated to all those who work hard at
keeping the memory of the past and
lost love ones alive - the
keepers of the flame.*

Many thanks to:

*David Perdue (confidant)
Curator of The Civil War Room in the
Jefferson County Historical Museum, Pine Bluff Arkansas*

*W. Danny Honnoll and M. Ray Jones
The Sons of Confederate Veterans, Jonesboro Arkansas*

*Paul Arnold
Curator of Stars and Stripes Museum, Bloomfield Missouri*

Thank God for the Gideons

*Village Creek Publishing, LLC
317 Main St. Swifton, Arkansas 72471*

CONTENTS

Title Page

Copyright

Dedication

Chapter 1 - The War's Over ... 2

Chapter 2 - Battle at Pea Ridge / Elkhorn Tavern ... 15

Chapter 3 - Arkansas Troops Exit Arkansas for Shiloh ... 24

Chapter 4 - Hindman - King for a Day ... 29

Chapter 5 - Mound City St. Charles, Cotton Plant & Helena ... 39

Chapter 6 - Marmaduke, Cane Hill and Prairie Grove ... 46

Chapter 7 - Arkansas Post, Old Tige, Chalk Bluff ... 56

Chapter 8 - Helena ... 70

Chapter 9 - Devil's Backbone & Yankees in the Capital ... 82

Chapter 10 - Pine Bluff & Hanged at 17 ... 99

Chapter 11 - The Red River Campaign ... 112

Chapter 12 - The Camden Expedition ... 127

Chapter 13 - Du Vall's Bluff, Jacksonport & Ditch Bayou ... 140

Chapter 14 - Price's Expedition & Anarchy in Arkansas ... 150

Chapter 15 - Dardanelle, Ivey's Ford, Appomattox & Mexico ... 160

About The Author ... 168

Hunter Jones

Joins

The Civil War

(Arkansas)

Note to reader --- Hunter Jones is a 12 year old orphan boy who gets sucked up into the Civil War. He winds up in the hospital in a deep coma from being kicked in the head by an Army mule. Two old-timers take a liking to him and visit him daily. While there they talk and discuss the war and its many battles and conflicts as they read about them in the daily newspaper. Hunter's imagination absorbs these conversations and his dreams carry him off to high adventures and exciting escapades. Through his dreams, we the reader get to see history and the Civil War from a different point of view, through the eyes of a 12 year old boy.

CHAPTER 1 - THE WAR'S OVER

(Hospital)

Abby's mother swooped into the hospital tent looking for Abby. "Miss Abington," she declared with a smile on her face. "You are right where I thought I would find you, reading poetry to that little Hunter boy."

Abby's mother was a woman small in stature but big and bright in her nature. She always had a ready smile and dancing blue eyes, and her dress was always smart and fashionable. She floated over to Hunter's cot and looked at the book Abby was reading from. "Ah, Walt Whitman, one of my favorites." She took the book and pressed it to her bosom. She was silent for a long moment then from memory recited: "From Drum Taps - Aroused and angry, I thought to beat the alarum, and urge relentless war; But soon my fingers fail'd me, my face droop'd, and I resign'd myself, To sit by the wounded and soothe them, or silently watch the dead." She stopped as a tear came to her eye. "Such a great poet and such a kind and considerate heart." She turned to Patch. "He's a Civil War nurse who helped doctor his brother George Whitman back to health after searching for him in the many hospitals set up in Washing D.C. Did you know that, Patch?"

"No, ma'am." Patch said, still standing after having immediately sprung to his feet when she walked into the tent. Peg was still struggling to stand.

"That's alright, boys." Abby's mother patted Peg on his shoulder and gently pushed him back into his chair. "I appreciate the chivalry of you fine Southern gentleman, but as war heroes, I should be standing for you." And she patted Patch on his shoulder and gently pushed him back into his chair, too. She turned her attention to Abby, "I knew I would find my little angel hovering over one of the South's fallen heroes." She turned to Patch and asked, "How is our little orphan Hunter doing? Poor thing lost his mom to measles and his dad to a stray bullet from a nasty riverboat gambler's gun."

"About the same, ma'am." Patch said, looking over at Hunter with concern.

"My husband said he'll remain in that coma until the swelling in his brain from that nasty old mule kick goes down." She hugged the book to her bosom as if it were Hunter. "The poor thing," she whispered, looking down at the sleeping boy. She looked into his quiet sleeping face for a long moment and then turned to Patch. "Are you boys taking good care of him?" She smiled at both of them.

"Yes ma'am." Peg offered quickly. "In fact, I'm taking better care of him than Patch is."

"I bet you are." She just smiled to herself as she handed Patch a new, neatly folded newspaper. "Here, the General just got this newspaper in this morning's mail. He's finished with it and asked if I would bring it over for you to read to Hunter?"

Patch eagerly took the newspaper and busied himself, scanning the headlines.

"Abby, tell Hunter and the boys goodbye. Your dad and the general are waiting lunch on us." Abby's mother turned to the two men as they started to get up. "Sit. Sit. Sit." She ordered warmly. "Abby can come back later and read some more poetry to Hunter, if you don't mind."

"It is always our pleasure, ma'am." Patch said, smiling over toward Abby. "Her poetry is comforting to a fallen soldier." He shot a glance over toward Peg and continued, "And it can take the edge off some knotty old pine, too."

Peg blustered up. But before he could say anything Patch continued, "Back when I lost my eye, I was in a coma for many weeks, and till this day I can still remember the things that went on around me and conversations people had. So I know the tender and caring words of your daughter's poetry touch Hunter's heart."

"Why, thank you, Patch." She patted Abby on the top of the head.

"And may I add," Patch said, lowering his voice and head slightly, "that beauty does not fall far from the tree."

"Patch you are too kind." She patted Abby on the top of the head more lovingly. "She's my little precious." She smiled at Patch, "I'll send her back with a different poet next time." They both started moving toward the exit. She turned back to Patch and said, "Patch, you keep reading the battlefield stories out of the newspaper to Hunter." She stopped and smiled at both men and continued, "The South will win this vile, loathsome war and soon." In saying that, they both disappeared through the exit.

Silence filled the room until Peg, with a wrinkled up face, snorted in a weaselly voice, "…and may I say beauty does not fall far from the tree." Peg, still with a wrinkled up face, started to repeat himself, but before he could, Patch held up a hand with its palm facing Peg and cooed, "A kind word, especially to a lady, is always warmly appreciated."

Peg spit a stream of brown juice into the brass spittoon and wiped his mouth with the sleeve of his shirt.

"I can see my sage advice has fallen on deft ears once again."

Peg put a cupped hand to his ear and honked, "Huh? I can't hear you."

Patch ignored his puckish friend and busied himself thumbing through the new battlefield newspaper.

"Arkansas' One Day War Is Over," Patch read the headline out loud. He folded the newspaper in half and searched for a more comfortable spot in his chair. "It says here on April 15ᵗ, three days after the Confederates captured Fort Sumter, President Lincoln called for 75,000 troops from each state to help get back the US property that the Rebels were confiscating."

"The war's over." Peg blinked and looked quizzically at Patch. "Read that again."

"That's what the paper says." Patch turned the printed page toward Peg so he could see the large black headlines. "Arkansas' One Day War Is Over," Patch confirmed calmly, as he casually took a little sip of his coffee. Then, he added, "I guess Arkansas Governor Rector said no, when he got the news that Mr. Lincoln wanted 75,000 troops from each state for 90 days to shut down the rebellion and get back the Union's property."

"What?" Peg insisted.

"Instead of sending southern brothers to fight southern brothers, Arkansas joined their southern brothers, seceded from the Union and started confiscating Arkansas' share of the Yankee's property located in Arkansas."

"Like the Arsenal in Little Rock, Arkansas' capital?" Peg asked.

"Exactly. And like the paper explained. They jumped the Arsenal so fast that the Union officer in charge was caught off guard. But when they sent the three steamboats up river filled with men from the newly formed Confederate Army, those Union soldiers at Fort Smith had enough time to pack-up and get out."

"And you say they captured both without a shot being fired?"

"That's what the paper said." Patch sipped a little more coffee. "Evidently, they floated back down river to a hero's reception along the river banks."

(Dream)

"The war's over! The war's over! The war's over!" The men were screaming and dancing a jig with each other on the deck of the Tahlequah as it slipped easily down the Arkansas River headed back to Little Rock.

Hunter watched in amazement as the crowds standing along the riverbank applauded, cheered and did their own little jig, careful not to push each other into the muddy river. It was a crazy scene. Women threw kisses, old men tossed flowers and children danced around falling down and giggling as the three warships, Lady Walton, Little Rock and Tahlequah slipped silently downriver, riding the muddy currents effortlessly.

Hospital)

"And the war is over?" Peg added.

"That's what the Arkansans thought." Patch said, smiling slightly to himself, "And they chose some pretty fancy names as they were forming their units and putting them on the ships, The Hornets, The Knights, The Invincibles, The Hunters and The Heroes."

"Wow, the Invincibles?" Peg questioned.

"And they steamed upriver with some pretty romantic ideas about war planted in their heads. Listen to what one fellow named Danley told them about the decision to go to war, 'Now that the 'overt act' has been committed, we should, I think, draw the sword and not sheathe it until we have a guaranty of all our rights, or such standards as will be honorable in the South.'"

"That doesn't sound overly romantic or naive, if you ask me," Peg said, getting a little red-faced and starting to buck-up a little. "I don't think this war has anything to do with slavery, as the Northerners would have you to believe. It's all about the right of each state to make its own decisions and NOT having some big central government telling it what to do, how to do it, when to do it and who to do it to."

Patch looked sideways at Peg and snorted, "Tell that to the black folks who are being sold by the pound that it ain't about slavery."

"Blah. Blah. Blah." Peg snorted and spit a stream of brown juice into the brass spittoon. "It doesn't matter anyways. The paper says the war's over."

"Not." Patch said, snapping the paper open and reading the headlines to himself.

Peg waited for a long moment then huffed. "Well? Mr. Hunter and I are waiting to hear about the news."

"Well, it looks here like the war isn't quite over yet." Patch cleared his throat and added, "In fact it is just getting started." He read the newspaper to himself for a moment then summarized, "When the South seceded, it called for volunteers to fight the North. The First Arkansas Infantry was sent to Virginia but arrived too late and missed the First Battle of Bull Run. But another unit of Arkansans helped fight and win a bloody victory for the South at the Battle of Wilson's Creek in

Missouri. That's where the first Arkansan to die in the Civil War got killed."

(Dream)

Hunter helped the other three men pick up the limp lifeless body and put it into the back of the black ambulance. The mules, nervous with the distant cannon fire, shivered in the cold summer rain and shuffled anxiously in their tight leather harnesses as they jostled the wagon a little forward, causing the four men to shift and stumble slightly. The rain was merciless, and for Hunter, who was hatless, huge torrents of rain ran down into his eyes and blurred his vision. Once the body was loaded, the four men stepped back as the ambulance pulled away. They turned and sloshed back through the mud to the dryness of the hospital tent, slipping and sliding as they went.

"Who was that guy?" Hunter asked the burly man standing next to him, trying to light his wet pipe.

"Lieutenant Weaver, Omer Rose Weaver. He helped me organize the Woodruff Battery. We were boyhood friends. In fact, the whole battery here is made up of boyhood friends from Little Rock. Omer and I attended the Kentucky Military Institute together. My dad is the editor of the Arkansas Gazette, and before the war broke out, he got Omer a job as a land surveyor for Governor Henry Rector." The big man turned his head away as he wiped a tear from his face.

"How did he die?" Hunter turned his face toward the open tent door and watched as the light from the tent sparkled off the raindrops sliding down the back of the black ambulance as it slowly disappeared, slipping and sliding down the dark muddy road. "He looked so young."

Mr. Woodruff, eager to share his friend's heroic story, puffed some smoke out of his wet pipe and bragged, "He was born 24 short years ago in Roseville and moved to Little Rock with his folks. He worked hard helping me put this battery together and was, in the heat of the conflict, helping an artillery crew when he was fatally wounded. He took a six pound artillery shell to the chest but hung on for six hours."

"Why did we put him into the wagon? Where's he going?" Hunter asked, confused. His natural curiosity took over the moment.

"I am taking him back to Little Rock where he will have a hero's burial at Mount Holly Cemetery."

(Hospital)

Peg sniffed loudly and spit a stream of brown juice into the brass spittoon and wiped his mouth with the sleeve of his shirt. "We whipped the Yankees at the Battle of Bull Run, and we whipped the Yankees at the Battle of Wilson's Creek. I bet our boys were ready to march up to St. Louis and whip the Yankees up there, too."

"Well, it seems our General Price, after the win at Wilson Creek, was ready to run the Yankees all the way back to St. Louis, but his fellow general, General McCullock, turned his troops south and marched them back into Arkansas instead."

"Why?" Peg looked blankly at Patch.

"He was called back to Richmond Virginia to explain to President Davis why he didn't press the attack. He offered some excuse about 'Missouri had not yet seceded, and he was not sure if his troops were legally in Missouri.'"

"What did General Price say about that?"

"He didn't. He and General McCullock stopped talking to each other after that." Patch sipped his coffee and continued, "It says here, while Price and his troops celebrated their victory at Wilson's Creek, hundreds of Yankee troops were being shipped into the port city of St. Louis. Soon, they were on a roll back toward Springfield. Price got the word of the impending snowball coming at him and left Springfield quickly and headed south toward the Arkansas border. Unfortunately, some fast moving Northern cavalry men caught up with the slow moving tail of the Price's column as it slipped across the border into northern Arkansas." Patch looked at the paper carefully. "It says here that the Union's First Missouri Cavalry tangled with the Confederate's First Missouri Cavalry at a place called Pott's Hill just over the Missouri line into Arkansas."

"Ah, brother fighting brother and father fighting son, so sad," Peg grumbled and absently scratched his wiry beard.

(Dream)

"I told you to go with him." Mr. Davis, commander of the Third Division of the Army of the Southwest, said and slapped Hunter on the shoulder with the side of his sword. "I don't want to hear

anything about measles or being kicked in the head by a mule. I want you to go with Mr. Ellis and Colonel Wright and run down those Rebels before they have a chance to cross over into Arkansas and dig in." Commander Davis paused for a second and then kicked Hunter's horse's rump viciously. "Go! NOW!" He bellowed.

Hunter quickly joined up with Colonel Ellis as they barreled through the difficult terrain, hot after the fleeing Rebels. Upon emerging from the worst of Cross Timber Hollow, in the Big Sugar Creek valley, Ellis' Union First Missouri Cavalry was almost on top of the Confederate's First Missouri Cavalry, and the two fought a fierce galloping battle along the narrow Telegraph Road.

Suddenly Colonel Wright grabbed Hunter's reins. "I told you to turn your horse around." Wright was fighting to get his horse stopped and turned around, too. Finally doing so, he hollered over his shoulder to his cavalry troops, "Everyone, turn your horses around. We have overrun the Confederate lines and have to turn around to redirect our attack."

Wright's cavalry command turned around and attacked the Rebel artillery unit they had just ridden past. The fighting was brief but vicious. The Rebel artillery unit got off some good shots before the Yankees swarmed over them. "Hunter," Wright hollered at Hunter, "and you six, put those Rebels under guard." Satisfied that the situation was under control, Colonel Wright rode away with the rest of his command to rejoin Colonel Ellis 'attack on the rest of the fleeing Rebel cavalry.

Hunter slid off his horse and looked around at the sprawled out Rebel soldiers. "What's wrong with you?" Hunter asked the soldier next to him. "What's wrong with all of you?"

"We are plum tuckered out." The man that Hunter was standing next to sighed, "The Yankees have followed us so steadily and closely since we left Springfield that we've had no time to rest, eat or sleep." Just as the soldier was saying that, two Rebels prisoners jumped up and ran off into the woods.

One Yankee cavalry soldier raised his carbine to shoot, but the two disappeared almost instantly into the thick brush. As he lowered his rifle, another Yankee soldier snorted, "Save your powder. These Southern soldiers are nearly unconquerable."

An exhausted Southern soldier lying back on a stack of cannonballs hooted, "Unconquerable, Unbeatable, Undefeatable and Unflinching."

Another Southern soldier sitting exhausted on a rock hooted, "Invincible and Insurmountable."

And another Rebel hooted, "Defiant, Fearless, Resolute, Stubborn and Dogged." With that, they all let out a weak yet resounding Rebel yell and fell back exhausted.

(Hospital)

"It says here that a skirmish at Big Sugar Creek was the first skirmish between Union and Confederate forces on Arkansas soil. It was also called the action at Pott's Hill."

"The first battle? Ah, man, and here I thought the war was over with." Peg scratched his beard thoughtfully. "Didn't the Rebels just parade victoriously down the Arkansas River back to Little Rock?" Peg asked quizzically.

Not answering Peg's question, Patch continued, "Peg, it wasn't a battle. It was the first skirmish, the first North-South action on Arkansas soil.

"Action, skirmish but no battle," Peg huffed.

"No. It says here that the Battle at Pea Ridge didn't happen until two weeks later, when General Van Dorn pounded his fist on the table and snarled, "Let's go kill some Yankees and drive them back to St. Louis – Huzza!"

(Dream)

Hunter stood at rigid attention and watched with the other honor guards as the ambulance rolled to a stop.

"Who's sick?" Hunter whispered to the young boy next to him who carried the company's colors.

"General Van Dorn. After he left Pocahontas, he fell into the Little Red River and has been fighting a fever for the last nine days."

Suddenly, the Sergeant Major rapped Hunter on the hand with his swagger stick, causing him to drop one of his drumsticks. And through the side of his tightly clenched lips, he snarled, "You magpies shut up and stand at attention."

Later, after the welcoming formation was over, Hunter went back to his duties of carrying coffee to the officers. As he waited patiently at the hearth for the water to come to a boil, he leaned in closer to the

flag bearer, who was assigned to help him, and whispered, "Why is General Van Dorn so mad?" Just as he asked that, General Van Dorn slammed his fist on the table and growled, "I could not believe my ears when I heard you fled from the Yankees, allowing the Yankee General Curtis to push you out of Springfield."

"Sir, we did not retreat," General Price spoke up quickly. "We withdrew from Missouri to join up with General McCullock's troops here in Arkansas.

"Balderdash." General Van Dorn looked over his shoulder at General McCullock and snorted, "Horsefeathers." He stood up and looked at both of his generals. Then, he suddenly slammed his fist onto the tabletop and snarled, "Let's drive General Curtis back to Missouri and make him wish he was the mayor of Keokuk, Iowa, again." He slammed his fist on to the tabletop and through gritted teeth snarled, "Then we'll go capture St. Louis – Huzza."

CHAPTER 2 - BATTLE AT PEA RIDGE / ELKHORN TAVERN

(Hospital)

"It says here that General Van Dorn's plan was simple. The Army of the West, as Van Dorn called his new command, with over sixteen thousand men and sixty-five cannons, would overwhelm the Federal Army of the Southwest, who only had only 10,250 men and 49 cannons, driving them back to St. Louis – then Huzza."

"What's Huzza and Who's Van Dorn?" Peg asked blankly.

'Huzza is another way of saying 'hooray'. And General Van Dorn is the senior officer President Davis put in command over the two non-talking generals, General Price and General McCullock.

"Huzza," Peg hooted.

Patch read quietly to himself and then added, "It says here that General McCullock came up with a really good idea. They found out from spies that the two halves of the Yankee troops had come back together and were dug in at Little Sugar Creek facing south waiting for the Rebels to attack. McCullock explained to General Van Dorn that the Old Bentonville detour would take them up and around the back of the Yankees. From there, they could attack from the north while the Yankees faced south. This plan would cut the army off from its supply line from Missouri, forcing them to surrender."

"I like that plan even better, Southerners attacking from the north," Peg bellowed, slapping his one good knee. "Once we have the Yankees gunpowder, weapons, mules and wagons, we can deliver this war right to St. Louis 'front door steps. Huzza."

"Yes and no. You have to understand and recognize the situation at the time. The newspaper explained that the first vote in Arkansas for secession failed. The eastern half of the state is all flat Delta land near the Mississippi River. Cotton, plantations and slavery rules politics there. But the northwester section of the state was in the Ozark Mountains, and neither farming nor slavery was big political issues up there. So that's why the first vote to leave the United States failed. But weeks later when Lincoln asked for 75,000 troops from each state, the second vote for secession passed quickly and with flying color, all except for Mr. Isaac Murphy, who voted to stay in the Union."

"And he was born and raised in the Ozark Mountains," Peg quickly added.

"No and yes. No, he was born in Pittsburgh, Pennsylvania, in 1799. Yes, as a young man, he moved to Fayetteville, which is in the Ozark Mountains. There he practiced law and was elected to government office. But my point is that since slavery was not a political issue for the folks in the Ozarks, the Ozarks was thick with Northern sympathizers and supporters who were ready and quick to warn General Curtis that the Rebels were splitting up their troops and were planning to come up from behind him."

"Fiddlesticks," Peg grumbled. "Yankee spies."

"The paper says it took all day for General Curtis, once informed, to turn his cannons around facing north and dig back in. But he did, and they were ready when Van Dorn, Price and McCullock came marching out of Bentonville." Patch sipped his coffee and continued, "All thanks to the Northern sympathizers."

"Spies," interjected Peg.

"Whatever. Thanks to the Northern sympathizers, Curtis knew that Van Dorn had split off McCullock's troops and sent them to Leetown in a flanking effort. Curtis in turn sent two

Yankee scouting parties to harass and slow the Southern troop's positioning efforts." Patch folded the newspaper back and continued, "At Leetown, McCullock, McIntosh, Hébert, Pike and his Indians got tied up with these Union troops, delaying their meeting up with Van Dorn and Price, who was waiting for them near the Elkhorn Tavern."

(Dream)

Hunter grabbed the Indian's knife hand by the wrist and pulled him up from his kneeling position. "What are you doing?" Hunter screamed over the thunderous burst of the cannon and musket fire. The smoke was thick, and his nose and mouth were filled with the taste of sulfur and black gunpowder. "What are you doing?" Hunter screamed again, this time right into the face of the Cherokee warrior - trying to be heard.

The warrior blinked at him quizzically and then pushed him away savagely. As he turned and bent back down to his business, Hunter sprang up out of the dirt and dust and jumped on the Indian's back before either one of them realized what he was doing. The Indian rolled over, out of his kneeling position, landing on top of Hunter.

The Indian sprang to his feet and wheeled around with the bloody knife in the ready position. He was quivering; he was so angry that his business got interrupted and by a mere boy at that. He poked his bloody knife savagely at Hunter's soft underbelly. Hunter sucked it in and moved back just in time. Now even angrier that this mere boy was besting a proven and accomplished warrior, he slashed at Hunter's face, first from the right and then from the left.

Even though Hunter was quick and agile and missed the stabbing slashes of the warrior in front of him, he didn't duck when another Indian hit him in the back of the head with the butt of his rifle. Hunter's eyes rolled back into his head. His knees buckled, and he dropped to the dusty ground like a ten-pound bag of freshly picked potatoes.

He must have lain there for a long time because when he finally did lift open his ten-pound eyelids, the deafening roar of the cannons were silent. The battlefield, dank and musty, was silent as well. And all around him was silent, except for an occasional sharp pop from a distant musket. The stench of sulfur still filled his nose, and the taste of black powder still filled his mouth. He raised his head up slowly and cautiously looking for Indians, but there were none. The only thing he could see were dark heaps of dead bodies wrapped in swirling stripes of gray smoke.

Still wary of an Indian attack, he slowly and watchfully rose up to a kneeling position. Nothing. He slowly stood up and cautiously looked around, just as a full moon began to rise like a copper disk over the horizon. He took a deep breath, held it and listened intently. Still nothing or nobody. He tried to get his feet to work, to move away from the nearest mound of dead soldiers, but he froze and blinked. He blinked his eyes again and again. No. He thought to himself. No. He shuffled and dragged his feet over toward the closest mound. He blinked his eyes again. His head started spinning as the air whooshed from his lungs. He wobbled around on his useless legs for a few steps before falling forward on his hands and knees. He looked down at the copper colored clods of dirt and threw-up.

(Hospital)

Peg rubbed his beard furiously in disbelief. "Indians!" He declared, rising slightly from his seat. "Indians? What kind of gentlemen's war is this when they make soldiers out of Indians?"

"It says here that General Pike signed a deal with the Five Civilized Tribes of the Cherokee Nation. The deal was that the Confederacy agreed to pick up the support payments that the US government had fallen behind on, agreed to deliver more guns and munitions and agreed that the Indians would only be used to harass and distract the Yankee troops, keeping them tied up in Indian Territory and unavailable to fight in other states."

"Indians," Peg said, still complaining.

General Pike

Gen. Chief Watie

"Another part of the agreement with Chief Watie was that the Indians would never, ever be used outside of the Indian Territory." Patch took a sip of his coffee and a tiny bite from his cinnamon roll before he continued. "It seems that before the ink could dry on the new agreements, Van Dorn had told Pike he needed his Indians to help him with the battle at Pea Ridge. Pike reluctantly complied, and the braves insisted on payment up front to their families before they rode the 80 miles from Tahlequah, Oklahoma, to Pea Ridge. Pike paid them with large sums of Confederate money."

"Other than the Indian stuff, how did our boys do?" Peg asked anxiously, moving closer to Patch.

"Not good. No, not good at all. After all the smoke cleared and the tallies were totaled, McCullock and his second in command, General James McIntosh, were killed near Leetown. Then Colonel Louis Hébert, the next in command, got captured on the back road leading to Pea Ridge. So, without a command structure, McCullock's foot soldiers fell back into the woods and did not press the battle."

"Now, don't tell me what happened next." Peg inhaled loudly, still perched on the edge of his chair.

"With the absence of McCullock's troops, Van Dorn and Price faired badly. The battle at Pea Ridge centered around the Elkhorn Tavern. Even though Curtis moved his cannons up from Little Sugar Creek to support his Yankee troops, the Union Colonel Eugene Carr's Fourth Division gave ground grudgingly to our General Price's superior numbers. In the late afternoon, the Missouri Rebels, led by Colonel Henry Little, pushed Carr's battered Fourth Division back from the area around Elkhorn Tavern, south to Ruddick's cornfield. Then, they moved east on Huntsville Road and dislodged the Iowans as nightfall ended the fighting."

"I thought you said Van Dorn and Price faired badly?" Peg scrunched up his face and fish-eyed Patch sideways and then added, "It sounds like our boys did a pretty good job of running off the Yankees if you ask me."

"The Battle of Pea Ridge would be decided the next day." Patch avoided the comment and continued reading. "The Yankees spent most of the night preparing. Even though almost half of the enlisted troops and many of the officers spoke German as their first language, General Curtis, nevertheless, successfully rearranged the Army of the Southwest and made sure the men were fed, rested, and supplied with ammunition. The next morning, Union troops were ready to resume combat, but the Confederates were not. Van Dorn needed to re-concentrate his army. In the process, he neglected to bring up the supply trains from Bentonville, so most of the Rebels did not get food or new ammunition. The next morning, the Federal cannoneers were relentless. Realizing he had lost and was in danger of being trapped and destroyed, Van Dorn sent his exhausted army east toward Huntsville." Patch paused for a second and then read a quote. "One Yankee soldier from Iowa said, 'It was a continual thunder, and a fellow might have believed that the Day of Judgment had come. The thunderous noise could be heard fifty miles away.'"

"Germans," Peg said thoughtfully to himself. "Wow." He murmured, slipping silently back into his chair, perplexed. "Wow, where did they come from?"

Patch avoided the obvious answer and continued reading. "The Battle of Pea Ridge cost the Yankees 1,384 casualties or roughly 13 percent of the 10,250 troops who came to fight in Arkansas. It's figured that the Confederacy had 2,000 casualties or 15 percent of the 16,500 Rebels, which included Pike's 800 Indians but not including the Creeks and Choctaws who arrived too late to fight."

"Germans." Peg looked quizzically at nothing. "And Indians," he added as he spit a stream of brown juice into the brass spittoon and wiped his mouth with the sleeve of his shirt thoughtfully.

"Yes, Germans and Indians." Patch looked at Peg and then back to the newspaper. "There wasn't much that President Davis could do about the Yankee Germans, but he could do something about the Indians. After the scalping incident hit the Southern newspapers, he ordered General Pike to take his Indians back to Indian Territory. And that was the last of the Indians being deployed in any significant numbers. It says that Chief Watie gladly went back to his original mission of harassing and distracting Yankee troops within the boundaries of the Indian Territory."

"What happened to Van Dorn?" Peg asked, absently pushing further back in his chair. He was obviously still wrestling with the idea of Germans and Indians fighting in a gentleman's war.

"Van Dorn went to Van Buren six miles north of Fort Smith and rested with his troops." Patch took a small bite of his cinnamon roll and a sip of coffee before continuing. "Interesting. General Beauregard sent a telegram to Van Dorn requesting his assistance and that of his 'Army of the West'. Wait!" Patch interjected. "I can see why. It looks like General Grant and his troops are in steamboats coming down the Tennessee River with plans to crush the rail crossing at Corinth, Mississippi."

"'Army of the West'. I like the way that sounds," Peg cooed to himself as Patch read quietly to himself for a moment.

"Well, don't get used to it. Wait until you hear this. General Van Dorn moved his men the 200 miles east to Des Arc and boarded steamboats headed down the White River to the Mississippi River and to Corinth. Unfortunately, Van Dorn's arrival was too late.

CHAPTER 3 - ARKANSAS TROOPS EXIT ARKANSAS FOR SHILOH

(Dream)

General Beauregard grabbed Hunter by the throat and squeezed. "What did you say, boy?"

A young lieutenant grabbed the general's wrist. "Sir, please. He's just a messenger." The lieutenant jumped to attention as the general loosened his hand slightly on Hunter's throat.

The lieutenant quickly delivered the message again himself. "Sir, General Albert Sidney Johnston has been hit in the leg by a stray bullet and has bled to death." Silence filled the air of the small church house. "You are now the supreme Confederate commander in the West." The lieutenant paused for a moment then asked, "What are your orders?"

"Attack!" General Beauregard huffed, absently squeezing Hunter's throat for emphasis.

"Attack?" The young lieutenant asked.

"Yes. Attack!" The general declared. "We surprised the Yankees here at the Shiloh Church and crushed their defenses at the Peach Orchard, Water Oaks Pond and the Hornets' Nest. Now we've driven them back past where they landed at the Pittsburg Landing. We will get up tomorrow morning and finish the job."

Hunter gurgled, trying to say something.

"What's your name, boy?" General Beauregard insisted with a squeeze.

"Hunter Jones, sir." Hunter gurgled. "I have the measles and was kicked in the head by a mule."

"What makes you think you have the measles? I don't see any red dots on you."

"My mother died from the measles."

Disgusted with the answer, the general squeezed a little harder.

"Just before General Johnston died," Hunter gurgled, "he told me to tell you that spies had told him that General Buell's Yankee Army of the Ohio was marching from Nashville to join up with General Grant and should be here by morning."

"Balderdash." General Beauregard hissed angrily and squeezed Hunter's throat until his eyes rolled back into his head, and he fell to the floor.

Hunter did not know how long he was out, but he came back to his senses as warm water tickled the back of his hand. He had to force his eyes open to see where the warm water was coming from. A huge black horse was standing next to him, relieving himself in the street. Hunter quickly scurried away from the flood, still holding the horse's leather reins. As he did so, he bumped into a young drummer

boy standing at attention. He too quickly snapped to attention and looked around blankly at the crowd of soldiers and civilians.

A tall, lanky officer stood in the box in the middle of the street that marked where the Memphis & Charleston and the Mobile & Ohio's railroad tracks criss crossed each other. Disgusted, he stomped his foot angrily.

Hunter leaned over and asked the young drummer next to him. "Isn't that General Van Dorn?"
The young drummer boy leaned away from Hunter and scrunched up his nose. "Geez, fellow, you smell like…."

"I know. I know." Hunter quickly wiped his hand on the back of his pants leg. "But why is he so mad?"

"He just read to us from the newspaper that the Battle of Shiloh in Tennessee produced 23,746 casualties out of 109,784 men engaged."

"Wow," Hunter said, absently wiping his hand on the back of his pants.

"Wow, that's right. The General said that the huge casualty list took both the North and South by surprise."

"I can see why he's so mad," Hunter said, testing the smell of his hand. He winced and tried wiping his hand even harder on the back of his pants.

"He's not mad about that. He just found out that the combined armies of Grant, Buell and Pope are ready to fall upon Corinth, and General Beauregard is pulling everyone back to Tupelo. The general is abandoning, without a fight, what Van Dorn calls the 'linchpin' of northern Mississippi."

(Hospital)

Peg spit a stream of brown juice into the brass spittoon and wiped his mouth with the sleeve of his shirt. "Read that again," he insisted.

"I said, unfortunately, Van Dorn's arrival with all of our Arkansan troops at Shiloh was too late for the battle. And with the absence of those impressive numbers and the reinforcements he got from General Pope and Buell's Army of the Ohio, Grant easily overran Beauregard's defenses and sent the Rebels fleeing the 20 miles south to safety at Corinth, Mississippi."

"Corinth. I've been there," Peg mused. "Two pairs of railroad tracks crisscross right in the middle of town."

Patch cleared his throat and continued reading. "Within 60 days, General Grant's Yankees had captured Memphis and Corinth, the 'linchpin 'of the south, where two pairs of railroad tracks crisscrossed right in the middle of town."

"Linchpin?" Peg said quizzically. "I thought a linchpin was a pin placed crosswise through an axle to prevent a wheel from falling off."

"That's it, something that holds things together to keep them from falling off or falling apart. I think that is what Van Dorn meant when he called Corinth the 'linchpin 'of northern Mississippi."

"For the want of a nail, a shoe was lost. For the want of a shoe, a horse was lost. For the want of a horse, a general was lost. For the want of a general, the battle was lost." Peg mused to himself and then added, "I guess that goes for Linchpins, too."

"Get this. More was lost than a nail or linchpin. Soon after Van Dorn arrived he became Commander of the Army of Mississippi."

"What happened to 'The Army of the West'?" Peg looked perplexed.

"That's the same question Rector, the Governor of Arkansas,

asked. He sent an angry message to President Davis telling him that, when Van Dorn left Arkansas, he took away nearly all horses, mules, weapons, ammunition, supplies and what little machinery the state possessed, leaving Arkansas almost completely defenseless."

Peg scrunched up his face and fish-eyed Patch. "Where's this Van Dorn fellow from anyway?" Peg asked as he spit a stream of brown juice into the brass spittoon and wiped his mouth with the sleeve of his shirt. "He ain't no Arkansan."
"No. It says here he was born in Claiborne County, Mississippi."

"Mississippi?" "Peg howled. "Get a rope."

CHAPTER 4 - HINDMAN
- KING FOR A DAY

(Hospital)

Abby sat next to Hunter's cot with two books in her lap. "I have two books by Washington Irving, *Rip Van Winkle* and *The Legend of Sleepy Hollow*." Abby opened the second book, cleared her throat and read. "The Legend of Sleepy Hollow is about Ichabod Crane, a stern schoolteacher and singing instructor who comes to Sleepy Hollow, New York, from Connecticut. It says here that he is lanky and sharp-featured, awkward and somewhat clumsy but more educated and sophisticated than the native villagers. He is quite fond of food and is well fed by the neighboring housewives, who share his delight in telling and re-telling ghost stories. When he sets his sights on marrying Katrina Van Tassel, it is not because of his feelings for her, but because her father is wealthy and Crane admires the food that is always displayed in the Van Tassel home. Katrina refuses him, preferring instead the manly and strong Brom Bones. Ichabod Crane, in his disappointment, falls victim to his own ghostly stories. On his way home from a dinner party, he passes through a dark, eerie forest, where he is chased by a headless horseman. The next morning, Crane does not come to school," Abby paused and looked over at the sleeping Hunter, "but you'll have to wait to find out how it ends."

She put that book down and picked up the other book. "Rip Van Winkle was written earlier in 1819 and published by Cornelius S. Van Winkle." She laughed at the publisher's name and continued talking. "It is about a fellow who falls asleep for 20 years and sleeps right through the American Revolution of 1776." She looked at each book in either hand as if trying to weigh them. "Let's read The Legend of Sleepy Hollow." She patted Hunter on the hand and added, "I bet you want to find out what happened to old Ichabod Crane, don't you?"

Patch punched Peg's good leg slightly. "Wake up Peg. Miss Abby is about to read a story." Patch turned to Abby. "Peg had to get up early this morning to slop the hogs and ain't been right since." Patch punched Peg's good leg slightly again. "Give him a little work, and he's plum tuckered out for the rest of the day."

"Hey, I can work circles around you," Peg challenged, as he got more comfortable in his chair and turned his attention to Miss Abby.

Miss Abby cleared her throat and read. "FOUND AMONG THE PAPERS OF THE LATE DIEDRICH KNICKERBOCKER. A pleasing land of drowsy head it was / Of dreams that wave before the half-shut eye / And of gay castles in the clouds that pass / For ever flushing round a summer sky."

Peg nodded off for a moment but then heard Miss Abby reading. "Ichabod Crane was tall, but exceedingly lank, with narrow shoulders, long arms and legs, hands that dangled a mile out of his sleeves, feet that might have served for shovels, and his whole frame most loosely hung together. His head was small, and flat at top, with huge ears, large green glassy eyes, and a long snipe nose, so that it looked like a weather-cock, perched upon his spindle neck, to tell which way the wind blew. To see him striding along the profile of a hill on a windy day, with his clothes bagging and fluttering about him one might have mistaken him for the genius of famine descending upon the earth, or some scarecrow eloped from a cornfield."

(Dream)

Suddenly, Peg saw a large shadowy figure sitting on a horse standing in the middle of the road just up ahead of him. The rider was headless, but Peg could just barely make out the shape of a severed head resting on the pommel of his saddle. Terrified, Peg turned and started to run as fast as his good and his peg leg would allow. The headless horseman chased him as he stumbled down the dark, dusty road moonlit road. Unable to escape, he stopped, turned and screamed. "Don't throw the head at me!" The last thing he remembered was the sight of the rider throwing the bloody severed head at him, being struck in the face by the flying object and being knocked unconscious to the ground. Peg lay there moaning.

(Hospital)

"Peg, you alright?" Patched grabbed for Peg as he moaned and almost slid out of his chair.

Peg pushed himself back into the chair and nervously adjusted his old sweat-stained hat. "Yes. Yes. I'm okay. I'm okay." He nervously adjusted his hat again and asked, "So what ever happen to old Ichabod Crane?"

"Nobody knows," Abby offered. "After his run in with the headless horseman, no one ever saw him again. Brom Bones married Katrina, and they lived happily ever after. End of story."

Patch looked at Peg more closely. "Hey, old timer, you okay?"

"I'm okay. I'm okay," he offered in a tight, squeaky voice. Shuttering a little in his seat, he cleared his throat and added in a much deeper voice. "I'm just not a big fan of ghost stories and all that scary stuff."

Just then, a black orderly leaned his head around the tent door and cleared his throat. "Miss Abby, your momma is wait'n for you's in her carriage."

Abby jumped up and patted Hunter on his sleeping forehead. "I'll see you boys later," she said over her shoulder as she disappeared out the tent door.

"Ghost stories," Peg said before shuttering a little in his seat again. "Who needs them?"

Patch looked at him a little sideways. "You okay?"

"I'm okay. I'm okay." Peg pointed at the newspaper and asked, "So, what happened after General Van Dorn took all the Arkansas troops out of Arkansas?"

Patch picked up the paper and read to himself for a second then said, "Well, it seems that President Davis told General Beauregard to do something. So, Beauregard appointed General Hindman as the new commander of the Military District of the Trans-Mississippi."

"Okay. Now we're getting someplace. What did Governor Rector have to say about that?"

"He was more than unhappy. Listen to this. When Hindman got to Little Rock and saw everything was missing, he instituted Martial Law and took control of the whole state, with

complete disregard for the state's government, its laws and constitutional rights. In effect, he became a little tsar."

"Tee-zar?" Peg looked perplexed at Patch.

"No. The 'T 'is silent. It's like 'are 'with a 'Z 'in front of it. Zare. A tsar is like a dictator, like a heavy-handed taskmaster." Patch read to himself for a moment then added, "He instituted a conscription act to enlist more soldiers and executed accused deserters."

"Wow," Peg muttered. "He executed accused deserters."

"In an effort to pull an army back together, he stopped and collected the Texas troops headed for Mississippi. He got Price's Missouri soldiers back from Mississippi and told General Pike to send any non-Indian troops back to Arkansas."

"It sounds like he was getting ready to go back into the business of war and getting ready to defend Arkansas and take it back from the invaders."

"And that's the good news," Patch interjected then added, "the bad news is he rang a bell that he could not un-ring and that one bad decision was to blow back into his face."

"Kind of like spitting into the wind?" Peg said, spitting a stream of brown juice into the brass spittoon. After he wiped his mouth with the sleeve of his shirt he asked, "What bell was that?"

"The 'Partisan Rangers 'bell," Patch answered. "He created a group of resistance fighters whose job was to pester, badger, hound, hassle and harass Yankee troop activities in any way, shape or form they could."

"And the problem with that is?" Peg pressed.

"They were unsupervised, unregulated and very quickly turned into roving bands of thugs, thieves and hoodlums praying on the Arkansans across the state, stealing hogs, horses, hay and anything to eat, ride or sell."

"Oops."

"Oops is right. And they did this all under the guise of being General Hindman's Partisan Rangers."

"Wow."

"But wait. I think we are getting ahead of ourselves." Patch turned the paper back a few pages and looked at Peg. "Remember Yankee general, Curtis? He was running our boys all over northwest Arkansas. After his victory at Pea Ridge, he pulled his troops out of Arkansas and parked them on the Missouri border near Rolla, waiting for what General Van Dorn was going to do next with his Rebel troops."

"Yes, the battle at Elkhorn Tavern," Peg said and spit a stream of brown juice into the brass spittoon.

"Pea Ridge," Patch said, turning his attention back to the newspaper. "Well it says here when General Curtis got wind that Van Dorn and his Rebel troop were on the move and moving east, he started moving his troop east along the Missouri-Arkansas border expecting anytime another attack into Missouri. However, when Curtis found out Van Dorn had moved his troop east, all the way across the Mississippi River into Mississippi, leaving Arkansas wide open and unprotected, he decided it was a good time to move his Yankees back into Arkansas. From West Plains, Missouri, General Curtis marched through Salem and 90 miles later was in Batesville, Arkansas. The trip was unopposed, and his troops were unmolested. At Batesville, he joined up with General Steele's troops and moved the 25 miles south to Jacksonport."

"Jacksonport? I've been there," Peg offered. "That's right where the Black River joins up with the White River. And together they flow down to the Mississippi River."

"Close, they flow down to the Arkansas River and six miles downstream 'it 'flows into the Mississippi River."

"Hey, I was close," Peg huffed.

"Close is only good in horseshoes and sawed off shotguns," Patch offered as he sipped his coffee.

"Whatever," Peg sniffed.

"Jacksonport is critical to the war efforts," Patch said, putting his cup down. "If you are in the eastern part of Missouri, you can jump on the Black River and be in Jacksonport in no time. The same is true if you are in the western part of Missouri. You can jump on the White River and be in Jacksonport in no time."

"And your point is?" Peg snorted.

"That is the point. Here all these Yankees flooded down the Black River and the White River and are now sitting in Jacksonport, Arkansas, with no place to go. So, General Curtis said let's march the 100 miles to Little Rock and capture the state's capital." Patch read quietly to himself for a moment and added, "This should get your dander up." Patch rattled the paper to get Peg's attention - who was busy fishing under his chair for his spittoon.

"It says here that Curtis 'ranks grew even larger when many Arkansans, who supported the Union, joined up with him in great and growing numbers."

"Ah, brother fighting brother and father fighting son, so sad," Peg mused. "This civil war is turning into an 'un-civil 'war if you ask me."

"Well, when they got halfway to the capital, his main body of troops stopped at the Little Red River near Searcy." Patch sucked his teeth for a moment and continued, "When Curtis got reports back that troops in his small foraging parties had battled the Rebs at Whitney's Lane, and those that had been captured were killed, some even hanged and their bodies mutilated by Hindmen's orders, he issued an order of his own, 'take no more prisoners of armed bandits.'"

"He may call them 'armed bandits', but I call them Partisan Rangers," Peg snorted.

"Hindmen's troops and his Partisan Rangers were doggedly harassing Curtis 'supply lines so relentlessly that Curtis decided to rethink trying to capture the capital." Patch pause for a second then continued, "It says here that Hindmen was not only successful with his troop efforts, but he was even more successful with his 'miss-information 'efforts. By the time he was through, he had Curtis believing that hordes of Texan troops were pouring into Arkansas, so in a knee jerk reaction, the general quickly pulled his Yankees back to Jacksonport and Batesville."

"Hindmen the hangman is going to drive Curtis to camp, to curl up and cry." Peg wiped his forehead and whooshed, "Wow, now that is some kind of.... What did you call it? I'm-about-to-pee-ah?"

"No. What you did is alliteration not onomatopoeia. Alliteration is the repetition of the same sounds at the beginning of words. Onomatopoeia is the use of words that imitate the sounds associated with something, such as hiss or bing, bong, bang, or buzz or murmur or 'as tinkling brass'," Patch said, rolling his eyes.

"What kind of 'constipation'?" Peg looked perplexed.

"Alliteration not constipation, but forget it." Patch snapped the paper and continued, "When General Curtis heard about Grant's success at Shiloh and that Corinth and Memphis had fallen, he asked for his needed supplies to be sent to him, not from Rolla but up the White River from Memphis instead." Patch waited for Peg to stop fooling with his hat then finally continued, "His request was quickly answered with a small flotilla of Federal gunboats and transports."

"Flotilla," Peg snorted. "Our boys are living off possum grapes and poke-salad, and we are still winning this war," Peg said huffing and puffing. "We don't need no stinking flotilla to win this thing; we've got guts and a burning desire to crush the Northern invaders."

Patch said nothing to the interjection but continued with his summary. "Well, it looks more like 'blow up 'the Yankees instead of 'crushing 'them."

CHAPTER 5 - MOUND CITY ST. CHARLES, COTTON PLANT & HELENA

(Dream)

Hunter grabbed the barrel of the sharpshooter's rifle and pushed it toward the ground as he screamed over all the firing. "STOP! STOP!" The sharpshooter looked over at Captain Frye with a blank look on his face. Captain Frye grabbed Hunter's wrist and pulled it away from the barrel. The sharpshooter went back to shooting the scalded men in the water trying to swim ashore. Hunter spun out from under Captain Frye's grasp. As he did so, Captain Frye smashed him between the eyes with his fist. Hunter melted to the ground like butter in a hot frying pan.

Later, as someone stepped on him, he rolled out of the way and tried to pry open his eyes to see who was doing all the shouting. "Report." An officer was insisting to the two Yankee soldiers holding Captain Frye. "Sir, from a crew of 175, only 3 officers and 22 men escaped injury. At least 82 men died from wounds or were scalded by the steam. The rest were killed by Confederate riflemen standing on the shore shooting down into the water." The Yankee soldier paused before continuing his report to his superior officer. "Commander Kilty, it was like shooting fish in a barrel, sir."

Commander Augustus H. Kilty turned angrily away from Captain Joseph Frye and looked at Colonel Fitch. "Colonel, you did a good job landing your troops down river, slipping up and silencing the Rebel artillery."

"Commander, I only wished we had done a better job. The Rebels

fired on our men in the water with grape and canister from their field pieces, murdering most of those who were attempting to escape." Colonel Fitch turned away from Commander Kilty to stare at Captain Frye and added, "Then, this Confederate captain turned his sharpshooters on our sailors."

Silence washed over the dusty and battle weary combatants until finally Commander Kilty turned away from Captain Frye in disgust. "Have the Captain's shoulder wound dressed and put him on the USS Conestoga for transportation to Memphis and court marshaling," he ordered over his shoulder as he walked away.

(Hospital)

"Read that again," Peg pressed.

"It says here, when the flotilla got to St. Charles, about 40 miles up from the Arkansas River, the lead ironsides, U.S.S. Mound City, took a direct hit. The lucky Rebel cannon ball went through an open gun port, ripped open the boiler tank and filled the boat with scalding steam." Patch paused to take a breath and continued, "It says the scene which ensued was horrible. Many of the crew, frantic with pain, jumped overboard, and some of them were drowned."

"Wow."

"Wow is right. It says that Captain Frye is accused of giving the command to shoot the struggling survivors as they tried to stay afloat or swim ashore."

"I'm sorry. That doesn't sound like something our officers would do," Peg murmured.

"Well the newspaper says he was 'accused.'" Patch read in silence for a moment then continued," It looks like more bad news for the flotilla trying to get supplies up to General Curtis 'men up in Jacksonport. The flotilla only made it up river another 40 miles before low water at Clarendon halted it. But instead of waiting for rain, General Curtis and his hungry men decide to march the 130 miles from Jacksonport to Clarendon. When they got there and got fed, he and his commanders decided to go the 60 miles east to capture Helena on the Mississippi River, instead of the 70 miles west to capture the state's capital on the Arkansas River."

"He was afraid of the 'hordes 'of Texan troops pouring into the state," Peg hooted and howled, as he clumsily spit a stream of brown juice into the brass spittoon. Then, getting serious, he leaned forward slightly and asked, "Hey, what's our Hangman Hindman doing during all of this flotillas and Yankee troop movement?"

"He tried to stop the Yankees before they could get to Clarendon and their supplies. It says here he dispatched General Rust and his troops to try and stop Curtis at a shallow ford on the Cache River near Cotton Plant."

(Dream)

"I said hold on, boy!" The young girl's horse swirled around not

wanting to go in the direction where the bullets were coming from.

"My name is Hunter Jones, and I have the measles and was kicked in the head by a mule." Hunter cleared his throat nervously and stuttered, clinging to her waist the best he could. "I think it would be best if I got down."

"Well, this is no mule, measles boy, so hang on."

"Wait. Wait," Hunter pleaded over her shoulder. "Where are we going and why?"

"We are going to run that Colonel Hovey out of my dad's cornfield, along with that rag-tag bunch of Yankees he recruited from among the students and faculty at the University of Illinois." As she said that, Fannie Hill kicked her horse with both heels, and it reared up on its hind legs before dashing off toward the cornfield. Hunter held tight to her waist to keep from falling backward off the horse. She followed the Rebels as they all went screaming into her father's cornfield near Cotton Plant.

(Hospital)

Patch cleared his throat and continued, "The fighting was in a cornfield at Parley Hill's plantation. A Texan reported that the Rebels attacked 'yelling like savages and swearing like demons.'"

"That Rebel yell will turn your blood to ice water in an instant," Peg yelped and slapped his good knee.

"Unfortunately, the Rebels were met with a hail of bullets and even more Yankees, as Colonel Hovey's 33rd Illinois Regiment was quickly reinforced by the 1st Indiana Cavalry."

"More Indians?" Peg complained.

"Indiana Cavalry, Peg, not Indian cavalry." Patch smilingly

corrected his friend and continued, "After the Rebel's failed effort at stopping the Yankees, General Albert Rust marched his men back to Des Arc, and General Curtis marched his men to Helena. It says here that the Yankee's march to Helena was unimpeded and a cakewalk. It says that hundreds of slaves were freed along the way and followed the Yankees to Helena. When they got there, they marched into the city without a shot being fired. Once there, with hundreds of freed slaves, the Yankees constructed high earthworks around the little port city. Helena became an important post for the Union army, serving as a depot to support operations against Vicksburg, Mississippi, and as a base to attack Rebel resources in the Delta."

"What did Hindman think about all that?" Peg asked, rubbing his beard nervously.

"Well, to add salt to insult, when General Curtis marched into the city of Helena, he also marched right into General Hindman's family home on Biscoe Street between Louisiana Street and Arkansas Street.

"What did Hindman think about all that?" Peg scrunched up his face and fish-eyed Patch sideways.

"Well, Hindman's career at being King of Arkansas was about to come to an end, having lasted only about 90 days. It says that Governor Rector was unhappy with the heavy handed way Hindman was running the state and complained bitterly and often to President Davis."

Jeff Davis President CSA

Theophilus Holmes (Granny)

"Like what?"

"For example, he was burning rich people's cotton to keep it from falling into the hands of the Yankees. He was killing poor people's animals and burning their corn crops to keep them out of the hands of the Yankees." Patch paused and read silently for a moment then added, "It says citizens even needed a pass to go from town to town or even across town to visit your sick mother." Patch looked up at Peg and added, "Well, anyways, the Governor complained to President Davis and even threatened to secede Arkansas from the Confederacy if something wasn't done." Patch went back to reading out loud, "It says that President Davis sent General Theophilus Holmes to take over command at Little Rock and demoted General Hindman back to a field officer.

"It sounds like Hindman did a pretty good job if you ask me," Peg offered.

"It wasn't WHAT Hindman did. I guess it was the WAY he did it that got all the civilians fed up with him and his tough-handed way of doing things," Patch said then added, "however, undaunted and still burning with hatred for the Yankees, especially those living in his family home at Helena, Hindman wanted to attack something, anything. So he came up with a plan to attack Missouri."

"Attack sounds good," Peg insisted.

"Not to the new boss. General Holmes didn't want to attack anything. With what few troops he had left, he only wanted to defend Arkansas and keep the Yankees out of the state, as best as possible."

CHAPTER 6 - MARMADUKE, CANE HILL AND PRAIRIE GROVE

(Hospital)

Abby picked up one of the books in her lap and read the author's name aloud, "William Cullen Bryant. He's an interesting American poet. It says here that the inspiration to write 'To a Waterfowl 'came to him one day when he was walking to work. He lived in Cummington, Massachusetts, and at the age of 21, he practiced law in Plainfield, seven miles away. He said he watched as a lone bird flew south and pondered the mysteries of migration and the bird's instinct to fly south for the winter." She cleared her throat and began to read: "To a Waterfowl, by William Cullen Bryant. 'Whither, 'midst falling dew, / While glow the heavens with the last steps of day, / Far, through their rosy depths, dost thou pursue / Thy solitary way? / Vainly the fowler's eye / Might mark thy distant flight to do thee wrong, / As, darkly painted on the crimson sky, / Thy figure floats along.'"

"What's a 'fowler's eye'?" Peg interrupted.

"A hunter, Peg, a hunter. Now, please be quiet," Patch insisted. "I'm sorry for the interruption, Miss Abby. Is there more to the poem?"

"Yes. It goes on for many more stanzas but I have so many books. Let's read another poem from Bryant before moving on." She leafed through the book and stopped on a new page.

"'Thanatopsis', his most famous poem, is Greek for 'meditation on death'. It has an interesting origin. It's told that his father, a poet too, took some pages of verse from his son's desk, and in 1817, he submitted them, along with his own work to a magazine. The magazine was impressed with the young 17 year old writer's work and professed, 'That was never written on this side of the water! 'meaning a young nation like America, what, 1776 to 1817, only 41 years old, could not produce quality poetry equal to that which was coming out of England."

"I guess they were still angry about losing the War of 1812, after burning down our White House. Thank you." Peg sniffed and rubbed his beard.

"Peg, can we stay focused?" Patch insisted. "Go ahead, Miss Abby."

"It says here that Mr. Bryant is responsible for translating the messages of 'English Romanticism 'into something new and very American. He gave Romantic poems a new voice, an American voice." Abby paused for a second then continued, "In 'Thanatopsis', Bryant is looking to nature for lessons about life and death. He tells the reader "When thoughts/Of the last bitter hour come like a blight... Go forth, under the open sky, and list / To Nature's teachings...""

Abby looked over the top of her book to check her audience. Then, she read aloud, "Bryant, it says here, wants the reader to slow down and smell the roses - to listen to nature's teachings and to contemplate nature's beauty. By contemplating his surroundings, the reader is able to develop both spiritually and morally and be better able to live his life to its fullest, so he does not have any regrets when he dies." Abby paused for a second then continued, "'Thanatopsis' plainly shows that truth can be found in the unspoiled beauty of nature." She turned the page and read: "To him who in the love of Nature holds / Communion with her visible forms, she speaks / A various language; for his gayer hours / She has a voice of gladness, and a smile / And eloquence of beauty, and she glides / Into his darker musings, with a mild / And healing sympathy, that steals away / Their sharpness, ere he is aware. When thoughts / Of the last bitter hour come like a blight / Over thy spirit, and sad images / Of the stern agony, and shroud, and pall, / And breathless darkness, and the narrow house, / Make thee to shudder, and grow sick at heart; -- / Go forth, under the open sky, and list / To Nature's teachings, while from all around -- / Earth and her waters, and the depths of air -- / Comes a still voice. -- / Yet a few days, and thee / The all-beholding sun shall see no more / In all his course; nor yet in the cold ground, / Where thy pale form was laid, with many tears, / Nor in the embrace of ocean, shall exist / Thy image. Earth, that nourished thee, shall claim / Thy growth, to be resolved to earth again, / And, lost each human trace, surrendering up / Thine individual being, shalt thou go / To mix forever with the elements…"

"Wait. Wait." Peg moved forward on his chair, complaining. "The last bitter hour come? Cold ground? Mix forever with the elements?" Peg rubbed his beard furiously and added, "Hunter ain't dead. He's only asleep." Peg rubbed his beard furiously again. "Can't we read some happy stuff? That 'mix forever with the elements 'stuff creeps me out. I can only imagine what it is doing to poor Hunter."

Just then, a black orderly leaned his head around the tent door and cleared his throat. "Miss Abby, your momma is wait'n for you's in her carriage."

Abby jumped up and patted Hunter on his sleeping forehead. "I'll see you boys later," she said over her shoulder as she disappeared out the tent door.

Peg turned to Patch and said, "The last bitter hour come? Cold ground? Doesn't that talk creep you out?"

"Take it easy, Peg, it's a poem," Patch said reassuringly, looking down at his newspaper.

Peg spit a stream of brown juice into the brass spittoon and shuttered a little in his seat. "Well, it does me." He snorted and shuttered a little in his seat again. "Let's get back to the business of war." He cleared his throat and pointed at Patch's newspaper. "Can't somebody talk to this new general in Little Rock, General Holmes, and say something to get him back into the war business?"

"Well, like they say, 'the best defense is a strong offense.'" Patch took a sip of his coffee and continued, "Somebody must have said something because the general's office put an attack plan into motion that put Mad Man Marmaduke on the move." Patch looked sideways at Peg and smiled. "Now, that is alliteration."

"I like – My Main Man Marmaduke is on the move." Peg sniffed.

"Whatever." Patch gave up the tussle and read out loud, "General Marmaduke led an advance guard of 2,000 cavalry soldiers from the Arkansas River valley up through the Boston Mountains of northeast Arkansas, en route to southern Missouri."

(Dream)

Hunter was bending over digging mud off the toe of his boot with a short stick when he was yanked backwards into a dark hallway and pulled down to the bricked floor. He had been sent to fetch fresh water but the mud on his boot had distracted him from his task.

"Shut up," a female voice whispered into his ear as another female's hand pressed hard against his mouth. "Who are you? Friend or foe?"

With eyes as big as saucers filled with white milk, Hunter lay on his back, looking around at the three young women holding him down on the brick hallway floor. "My name is Hunter Jones. I've got the measles and was kicked in the head by a mule," he mumbled around the girl's hand the best he could.

"He don't talk like no Yankee," one of the girls giggled as she

uncovered his mouth. Another girl leaded in and in a hushed voice whispered, "We have a message for General Marmaduke."

"Who are you?" Hunter asked, trying to squirm himself into a sitting position and trying to look at all three girls at the same time. "Spies?"

"We are students here at Cane Hill College," the girl with the hushed voice answered.

"I'm majoring in drawing." The girl giggled again, as she covered her mouth this time. "I'm majoring in embroidery and painting," the girl kneeling in front of Hunter offered.

"We are all majoring in Moral and Mental Science," The girl with the hushed voice offered. "As girls, we are only allowed to be taught the basics in English and Mathematics here at the seminary. But enough of that, we have an important message for General Marmaduke. Tell him General Blunt has 5,000 Yankees with 30 cannons stationed near here."

(Hospital)

"Read that again," Peg insisted.

"General Marmaduke's advance guard of 2,000 cavalry soldiers bumped into 5,000 Yankees with 30 cannons at Cane Hill, about seven miles south-west of Prairie Grove."

"Wow."

"Wow is right." Patch took a small sip of his coffee and continued, "The running battle between the two forces started near Cane Hill College and lasted for over nine hours and stretched over 12 miles of forested ridges and valleys. The Confederates were clever. Every time General Blunt's Yankees would set up their cannon for another round of cannonading, the Rebs would pull back just far enough to cause the Yankees to have to break down their cannons and move them up to a new line of deployment." Patch took a sip of coffee and continued, "This kept the Yankees addled enough for the Rebs to set up an ambush. The Southern troops withdrew down the mountain into the nearby Cove Creek Valley. Believing that the Confederates were on the run, Union cavalry stormed after them and charged headlong into a carefully laid ambush." Patch put his coffee cup down. "Taking advantage of a narrow pass formed by Cove Creek and a rocky bluff, Southern troops stunned attacking Federals, charging down Cove Creek Road. The Union forces fell back in disorder."

"It looks like we won another battle," Peg cooed.

"Almost. By now, night was falling, and under a flag of truce, the Southern officers asked if they could have time to remove their dead and wounded. They did, but during the night, Marmaduke wisely withdrew his troops back over the Boston Mountains to Dripping Springs, bowing to the superior number of enemy troops and cannons."

"I bet Hindman was hopping mad about all that?"

"No. In fact, he was happy. General Blunt and his Yankees had now been pulled even further into Arkansas and even further away from their supply lines up in Springfield, Missouri. General Hindman waited 9 days for supplies. Then, he put his 11,000 men and 22 cannons on the move. His plan was to move his troops around Blunt's northeastern flank, cutting him off from Springfield and food and driving him west into Indian Territory and the waiting guns of Chief Watie's Indian soldiers."

"So, what happened?"

"Hindman knew he could move his 11,000 men the 70 miles from Fort Smith to Cane Hill and crush General Blunt faster than General Herron could move his 7,000 Yankees 110 miles from Springfield Missouri to Cane Hill and reinforce Blunt's 5,000

Yankees."

Peg grunted. "70 miles? I can do that on one leg, in one day."

"Right." Patch sipped his coffee before he continued. "It took Hindman three days to move his troops over the Boston Mountains and into position at Prairie Grove and set up his command post in the Borden house. But before he could fall on Blunt's troops, Herron's troops marched up over the horizon."

"I thought you said Herron was 110 miles away," Peg grumped.

Borden house - Prairie Grove

"So did Hindman. But General Horron had forced marched his men 35 miles a day and made the 110 miles in only 3 days." Patch read silently for a moment then continued, "It says that only 3,500 Yankees survived the forced march. Many dropped out from exhaustion and bloody, blistered feet. When they arrived, they immediately attacked Hindman's vastly superior force. This was a mistake. The weary, footsore Yankee soldiers made two heroic assaults up the hill but were driven back with terrible losses. But just as Herron was about to be defeated, Blunt, ten miles away, heard the cannons and came to Herron's rescue."

"Man, 110 miles in three days?" Peg said to himself

"As the day wore on, more stragglers continued to swell the Yankee's ranks. The Rebels fought their hearts out, but Northern artillery, with exploding canisters and grapeshot, ruled the day. Every time Hindman's men would try to attack Herron on the right, Blunt's cannon would harass them from the left. And every time Hindman's men would try to attack Blunt on the left, Herron's cannon would harass them from the right. The Rebels, however, did not give up. They continued to attack and fight until nightfall. But under the cover of darkness and low on ammunition, the exhausted Rebels finally fell back to the safety of the Boston Mountains." Patch read for a moment then added, "Here's an interesting fact. Blunt's army includes several hundred Union Indians, some of whom fought briefly on the Confederate side at Pea Ridge nine months earlier."

"Indians from Indiana or from Indian Territory?" Peg joked.

"Well, all laughing aside, casualties on both sides were heavy at Prairie Grove. The Union forces of Blunt and Herron lost 1,261 killed, wounded, and missing; about 1,500 Confederates suffered the same fates."

"Well, at least our boys are safe on the other side of the Boston Mountains," Peg mused to himself.

"You wish." Patch interjected. "It says after Herron's and Blunt's troops rested, they marched the 70 miles south to Van Buren and attacked Fort Smith at the mouth of the Arkansas River. General Hindman and his Rebel troops were caught off guard and scattered, leaving their sick and wounded in the Fort Smith hospitals."

"Oh great." Peg sniffed and spit a stream of brown juice into the brass spittoon and wiped his mouth with the sleeve of his shirt.

"Once the Yankees burned all the supplies they could not carry, they withdrew back across the Boston Mountains and back toward Missouri." Patch paused then added, "Anarchic prevailed."

"Anarchic prevailed?" Peg wrinkled up his nose and repeated, "Anarchic? What's that?"

"The breakdown of law and order with no respect for established institutions, authority, rules or regulations. It says here that thugs, hoodlums and thieves, masquerading as Partisan Rangers, roamed Arkansas 'northwest. And soon patriotism deteriorated into a desperate struggle for survival against barbarism."

(Dream)

"Shut up and dig." With that, the fellow hit Hunter on the shoulder with a broken board six inches wide and almost three feet long. The fellow was nasty looking. He had an old ragged Rebel gray jacket on with Yankee blue pants. His hair was a tangled mess under an old, dusty Yankee forager cap. His brown, broken and missing teeth were hardly noticeable, hidden within a face full of tobacco-juice-stained and matted beard. "Dig, I said." Hunter could see his teeth as he scowled, so close he could smell his whiskey breath laced with fresh garlic chewed off uneaten pieces he had stuffed in his pockets.

"But what are we digging for?"

"That Caldonia Borden's folks think they are smart burying their food and belongings out here in the cemetery, but they ain't. They shape the fresh turned dirt on top like a grave, but we got on to that trick after a while. Now, we're digging up any and all fresh graves." He scowled a toothy scowl at Hunter and ordered, "No more questions. Just dig." He laughed to himself and added, "Once some Bushwhackers found a barrel of whiskey." He spit a stream of brown juice onto the dirt where he wanted Hunter to dig and wiped his mouth with the sleeve of his shirt. "I don't care anything about the Borden's meager belongings. I'm looking for their food." He paused then added, "But I'll drink their whiskey if we find any. Now dig."

CHAPTER 7 - ARKANSAS POST, OLD TIGE, CHALK BLUFF

(Hospital)

Patch looked to see if Peg was listening and continued, "It seems while Bushwhackers, Jayhawkers and other 'crazies 'controlled things north of the Arkansas River, the Southern generals still controlled things south of the Arkansas River and were still vigorously fighting a war." Patch read a moment and continued, "Granny Holmes, as Hindman's replacement was tagged, was worried about an attack on Little Rock, so he assigned Colonel Dunnington to take 3,000 troops down river 117 miles to the Arkansas Post and dig in. He did. He dug in and waited. But General Churchill, who was soon rotated in to replace him, didn't want to sit back and wait for anything. He wanted to attack something, anything."

"Good man." Peg rubbed his beard furiously and huffed, "Let's get a stick and put some whop on those Yankee yahoos."

(Dream)

The young drummer boy playfully tapped a few beats with his drumstick on Hunter's back as Hunter looked thoughtfully out across the muddy Mississippi, leaning on the wide railing of the huge steamboat. "What's wrong with you boy?" The young drummer boy playfully tapped a few more beats on Hunter's back. "Our Charging General Churchill just put a major hurt on those Yankees. Look at all that coal. Someone said that one barge was full of gunpowder and that the other barge had coffee, flour and fresh honey." The young boy licked his lips loudly as he playfully nudged Hunter. "What's wrong? Oh, that's right... you've been kicked in the head by a mule."

"This ain't got nothing to do with measles or mules." Hunter turned and looked at his playful young friend. "I'm just thinking how mad the Yankee generals are going to be when they find out all this stuff is missing. You talking about fresh honey, those Yankees are going to be on us like a thousand angry bees."

(Hospital)

"Read that again," Peg insisted

"To fulfill his desire to attack something, anything, General Churchill sent his troop down river 50 miles to the Mississippi. There they stumbled into and captured the huge Yankee steamer Blue Wing and the two barges it was towing filled with ordnances, supplies and coal."

"Man, finally some good news." Peg spit a stream of brown juice into the brass spittoon and wiped his mouth with the sleeve of his shirt.

Patch read for a moment then said, "Not so good." Patch paused. "Give me a second to read this again. I can't believe this," Patch said thoughtfully to himself.

"What? What?" Peg pressed impatiently.

"Are you ready for what the Yankees did in response?" Patch adjusted the newspaper and read aloud. "In response, the Yankee General McClernard sent William Tecumseh Sherman to attack Arkansas Post. Sherman, in 60 transports, took with him 32,000 infantry, 1,000 cavalry and 40 cannons. The flotilla, along with 3 ironclads, several rams and gunboats, which had been stalled for many months near Vicksburg, now lumbered silently up the Mississippi River and turned stealthily into the Arkansas River. Its mission was one: to 'destroy the annoyance 'at the Arkansas Post, which had been renamed Fort Hindman by General Hindman, and two: to open the way up the Arkansas River to Little Rock."

Peg rubbed his good leg nervously and mused, "32,000 to 3,000?" He looked like he was calculating in his head then added, "Wow, that is 10 to 1. Man, they are going to run over us like a June bug under a rusty old wagon wheel."

"You would think." Patch popped the newspaper noisily and added, "But listen to this. It took the Yankees two long days of constant bombardment by the Union navy to finally silence the Rebel artillery at the Arkansas Post. The outnumbered Confederate infantry finally did surrender but only after two days of defiance against overwhelming odds."

"Overwhelming odds!" Peg stomped his good foot in defiance. "The Yankees may have more men and materiel. But they'll learn you can't capture a man with two hearts, one for his body and one for his country," Peg said, sliding defiantly back into his chair and cocking his dusty old hat rakishly over one eye.

"Union casualties were 134 killed, 898 wounded and 29 missing." Patch continued to read, "The Confederates lost 60 killed, 80 wounded and 4,791 troops were taken captive and sent up the Mississippi River to be held at prison camps. The defeat cost the Confederate Arkansas Army nearly one-fourth of its troops."

"One-fourth?" Peg gasped.

"The article goes on to say that the Yankee General McClernard had issued orders for the massive number of Yankee troops to move up the Arkansas River and capture Little Rock. But General Grant rescinded the orders and had all the Yankees turn around to help him attack Vicksburg, Mississippi. It seems Vicksburg was more important to the total war effort than was the capital of Arkansas." Patch paused then mused to himself for a moment, "I guess opening up passage on the Mississippi River all the way from St. Louis down to New Orleans and out to the Gulf of Mexico really is much more important to the Yankee's Anaconda War Plan than is little old Little Rock." He sipped his coffee and added, "If you can strangle the South into submission and surrender, who needs the capital of Arkansas?"

Not listening to what Patch was saying, Peg mumbled to himself, "One-fourth?" He looked away as a tear slipped from the corner of his eye and whispered again to himself in disbelief, "Man, one-fourth!"

Patch put the paper down in his lap and sipped on his coffee, giving Peg a moment of silence. "Oh, look," Patch said, trying to be upbeat and pointing to a small headline at the edge of the battlefield newspaper. "It looks like the war is not over for the Rebels in Northwest Arkansas after all." He picked up the paper and held it closer to his face, so as not to look at Peg. "It looks like some 36 year old general, under the cover of darkness, with 900 Rebel soldiers, rode the 60 miles north from a little town called Ozark to Fayetteville where he caught the Yankee soldiers off guard."

"A 36 year old general?" Peg pressed quizzically

William Tecumseh Sherman | Gen. Cabell - Old Tige

"That's what it says. General William Cabell, they called him 'Old Tige.'"

"Old!" Peg snorted. "Thirty-six ain't old. I've got sweat stains in my hat older than that." Peg snorted again and spit a stream of brown juice into the brass spittoon and wiped his mouth with the sleeve of his shirt.

"Hum, I bet you do and maybe some in that shirt, too," Patch said, not lifting his eyes from the paper.

(Dream)

Hunter was laughing out loud as he leaned back on the back two legs of his wooden chair. He was about to wipe a tear from his eye just as the front door burst open and a shotgun blasted a hole in the stuffed deer head above the fireplace. Hunter's chair toppled over backwards. As it did, he rolled head-over-heels backward towards the fireplace. He lay on the floor, on his back, for no more than a heartbeat, but just as he was about to jump up, someone ran by and stepped on his open hand, pinning him momentarily to the floor. The room quickly filled with smoke and chaos as more shotguns exploded and more Rebel troops flooded into the small room through the front door. Women were screaming, and men were ducking and running. Hunter quickly jumped up off the floor. But just as he was getting ready to pick a direction to run, someone pushed him through a closed window. As they both fell to the ground outside, 'the someone' got up and escaped into the dark woods leaving Hunter flat on his back on the muddy ground with the wind knocked out of him, gasping for the next breath.

(Hospital)

"Read that again," Peg insisted

Patch cleared his throat and began to read again, "The Rebel column quietly approached the private house of a Union sympathizer. The Yankee soldiers inside were drinking, singing and dancing. When the Rebels burst in the front door with guns blazing, some Yankee soldiers scattered into the woods outdoors and windows, while others hid in cellars and under the floor of the house. The Yankee officer in charge was caught trying to hind up the chimney."

"You get'um, Old Tige," Peg snorted and slapped the knee of his good leg.

"He did. Come sunrise, his 900 troops fell on Fayetteville catching everyone in their nightclothes. His troops were busy shooting at anyone who ventured out of their quarters, while his two cannons on a hill top pelted the town with fused canisters and grape shot."

"Old Tige will make you think the war is over in Northwest Arkansas," Peg railed. "Anarchy? Balderdash! Our rebellion was just on temporary hold in that part of the woods." Peg laughed. "Com'on. Tell me the good news. "What happened? Did Old Tige run the Yankees back to Missouri?"

"Not quite. The battle raged on for four hours, but the Yankees had better rifles than our boys did and turned it around. Our boys were fighting with Arkadelphia rifles, which was nothing more than a shotgun, while the Yankees had the new longer-range Springfields and Whitneys." Patch paused for a second then asked, "Are you ready for this?"

Peg scrunched up his face and fish-eyed Patch suspiciously.

"The troops involved at the battle at Fayetteville were the First Arkansas Cavalry and the First Arkansas Cavalry." Patch looked at Peg for a second then added, "Two different cavalry units from the state of Arkansas one filled with Confederates and the other filled with Yankees."

"Brother fighting brother, neighbor fighting neighbor." Peg looked away and whispered almost to himself, "This is an UN-civil War."

While Peg continued mumbling to himself, Patch read quietly to himself and then offered, "While 39 year old Old Tige was busy with the business of war in the Northwestern part of the state, A 29 year old brigadier general was busy with the business of war next door, in the Northeastern part of the state."

"A 29 year old brigadier general?" Peg looked quizzical. Then a smile crept across his face. "My main man Marmaduke is on the march again."

"Correct," Patch said, a smile creeping across his face also. "It seems after the battle at Prairie Grove, the Yankees pulled most of their troops out of Arkansas and consolidated them back up in Springfield, Missouri. When they did, Marmaduke's cavalry flooded back into the Northeastern part of the state at Jacksonport and Batesville."

"And?" Peg said, holding the brass spittoon but not spitting.

"And, at Batesville, Marmaduke gathered 5,000 cavalry men.

And, turning them toward Missouri, he marched them the 170 miles north to Bloomfield, Missouri."

"Alright! Go put the 'duke 'on them Marmaduke," Peg said, putting down the spittoon and slapping his good knee.

"Put the 'duke 'on them Marmaduke?" Patch interrupted. "What does that mean, Peg?"

"I don't know." Peg rubbed his beard furiously. "But it sounds good. Put the 'duke 'on them Marmaduke. Put the 'duke'. Put the 'duke.'"

Patch had stopped listening and was reading to himself. "Listen, 1,000 of Marmaduke's men had no weapons, and 900 had no horses."

"Who needs weapons when you have the South in your heart?"

"It says that Marmaduke was from a politically prominent Missouri family and felt confident that the many Southern sympathizers in his home state would swell his ranks once he got there, and in sheer numbers, they could swamp the Yankees and continue to fight with captured weapons and munitions." Patch paused and looked sideways at Peg.

"Okay, Okay. You are giving me that look," Peg said, spitting a stream of brown juice into the brass spittoon. "What happened?"

"General John McNeil was in charge of the Bloomfield Yankees. The Southerners up there hated him because of his brutalities against Southern sympathizers living in Missouri and were eager to go up against him."

"Okay. But I feel a big 'but 'coming on." Peg squinted his eyes at Patch.

"But he ran. Instead of standing and fighting, General John McNeil pulled his troops out of Bloomfield and made a mad-dash the 50 miles east to Cape Girardeau, a busy port on the Mississippi River." Patch took a sip of his coffee and continued, "Marmaduke's superior cavalry troops fell on the Yankees at Cape Girardeau and held the attack until they were finally driven back by unrelenting cannonading."

"Cannons," Peg grunted to himself.

"Yes, but more than just cannonading. Marmaduke got word that Yankees were flooding into Cape Girardeau's back door from Cairo, Illinois, only 33 miles down river. He found out that more troops were coming down the Ohio River while even more troops were coming at him from Springfield, Missouri. Not wanting to get pinched between Yankee forces moving from different directions, Marmaduke wisely started moving his troops south, back toward Arkansas, down the Old Military Road."

"Did you know that the Old Military Road is built atop Crowley's Ridge, a ridge that extends from that Cape 'Gur-are-doe '150 miles down to Helena, Arkansas?"

"How do you know that?"

General Marmaduke

Jeff Thompson - Swamp Fox

"I've been on it. It's about 300 feet high, and all you can see for miles is wet delta land on either side of it." Peg straightened his hat smartly and proudly pushed himself back in his chair.

"Thank you for that little travel tip," Patch said, sipping from his coffee and avoiding Peg's pretenses. "Well, the Old Military Road is how Marmaduke kept his troops high and dry as they moved along it in an orderly fashion back to Arkansas. At Chalk Bluff, they would have to come down the ridge and cross the St. Francis River, knowing this Marmaduke sent some troops ahead to build a floating bridge out of logs."

(Dream)

Hunter was standing in mud up to his ankles as the rope mysteriously dropped over his head and fell to his shoulders. The officer on the raft was screaming something at him as he jerked on the other end of the rope. "Pull the rope, boy! Pull!" the officer screamed again.

Hunter grabbed the rope off his shoulders and started pulling. The crude, hastily constructed raft, made from fallen trees, slid effortlessly out of the water and up to the bank were Hunter was standing. The officer jumped off the raft as Rebel soldiers quickly jumped on to the raft to unload the cannons that were tied down. "Thank you, son," Jeff Thompson said, patting Hunter on the back. "That's my 20th and final trip back and forth across the St. Francis. Now, all of our cannons are safely back in Arkansas."

Hunter stood with his mouth open staring at the officer. Finally he blurted out, "Aren't you General Jeff Thompson, The Swamp Fox of the Confederacy?"

Before he could answer, a Yankee bullet zinged between them and cut in half the end of the rope Hunter was still holding. Just as they were about to drop to their knees, a young officer grabbed General Thompson and said, "Follow me sir. We have handpicked 200 rifle men to drive back the Yankees on the other bank, and you are right in their line of fire." As he said that, the bank on the Arkansas side roared with thunderous reverberations while angry hot sparks from 200 sharpshooters rifles 'spewed out across the rushing river waters toward the Yankees on the Missouri bank. Soon, boiling black smoke filled the air as the Rebels watched the Yankees scatter and as a Yankee officer's horse collapsed and died under him.

(Hospital)

"Read that again," Peg requested.

"It says here that 8,000 Yankees were pressing in on the Rebels, so Marmaduke's men had to hazard walking across the hastily built floating bridge by torch light in the dead of the night. The bridge was so rickety that the men had to walk across it in single file. Heavy cannons had to be ferried across on quickly made rafts while horses had to swim across the fast moving current. Many exhausted draft animals didn't make it and were found dead downstream the next morning."

"Man, that had to be scary, walking across that thing at night in torch light," Peg waxed thoughtfully.

"It got even scarier. When what they thought was the last man to cross, the Rebels cut the ropes made from grapevines and let the floating bridge be carried off downstream by the fast moving current."

"The last man had not crossed?"

"No. When 250 Texans who had been fighting a rearguard got to the river the next morning, the bridge was gone. So Lieutenant "Buck" Walton rode his horse headlong into the rushing water, and his men followed. The Yankees cavalry were right on their heels with slashing sabers and blazing pistols. The main body of Marmaduke's troops was now safely on the Arkansas side and atop the 70-foot Chalk Bluffs. They opened fire with their cannons as two hundred hand picked Rebel riflemen sniped at the pursuing Yankees. General McNeil's horse got shot out from under him as the Yankee cavalry quickly turned and disappeared back into the Missouri woods.

"Who won?" Peg pressed.

"The Rebels successfully stopped the attacking Yankees and turned them around at the Battle of Chalk Bluff, but the Yankees successfully stopped and turned around Marmaduke's raid into Missouri and his attack on Cape Girardeau on the Mississippi."

CHAPTER 8 - HELENA

(Hospital)

Abby shuffled through the stack of books in her lap and pulled out a dark brown one. "Ralph Waldo Emerson," she said, looking at the cover. "He's an interesting fellow. Mother said she read a newspaper article that he was anti-slavery. She said he voted for Abraham Lincoln in 1860 but was disappointed that Lincoln was more concerned about preserving the Union than eliminating slavery outright. Emerson made it clear, once civil war broke out, that he believed in immediate emancipation of the slaves. Emerson said 'The South calls slavery an institution... I call it destitution... Emancipation is the demand of civilization'. She said that the article pointed out that once he met Lincoln at the White House, his misgivings about Lincoln began to soften."

"Well, mine ain't softened any," Peg said, swelling up a little. "This war's about state's rights and stopping big government from telling us little people what to do and when to do it – period!"

Abby waited patiently, familiar with Peg's political position. When he fell silent, she looked over at Patch, who smiled and nodded her on. "It says here an important literary milestone in Mr. Emerson's career was an address he gave at Harvard in 1837 entitled 'American Scholar'. It says that, when many in the United States remained in awe of European culture, he argued that Americans were self-reliant enough to develop a literature reflecting their own national character. 'Our day of dependence, our long apprenticeship to the learning of other lands, draws to a close, 'he told his Harvard audience."

"I think Mr. Emerson is right," Patch offered. "I think we have some strong and powerful literary giants here in America." Patch stopped and jokingly cleared his throat. "Well, they may not be giant, giants but they ain't pygmies either." Patch looked at Peg. "You remember reading *The Last of the Mohicans*, don't you?"

Peg wagged his head no.

"Well, James Fenimore Cooper wrote *The Last of the Mohicans* in 1826. I loved it. He was among the first of our writers to appreciate the value of the frontier as a distinctly American literary setting." Patch slapped Peg's good knee lightly and added, "And you don't have 'that 'in Merry Old England. Why? Because they don't have a frontier." Patch slapped Peg's good knee again lightly. "Cooper created a masterful body of work that celebrated the courage and the adventure of the American character and explored the conflict between the wilderness and the advance of civilization." Patch paused and looked at Peg's blank face. "Cooper created a memorable frontiersman named Natty Bumppo, and in the process, portrayed nature as something to be used but protected and not conquered." Patch turned from Peg's blankness and looked hopefully at Abby.

Abby smiled and said, "I've read *The Deerslayer* and loved Natty's adventures."

"Thank you, missy." Patch turned to Peg and said, "Peg if you would read something more than the labels your 'chaw 'comes wrapped in you would know who James Fenimore Cooper is, or was. He died in 1851. The same year that Poe died."

Abby cleared her throat quietly. "Mr. Patch, Edgar Allan Poe died in 1849 at the age of 40. He wrote his famous poem 'The Raven' just four years before he died." Abby sweetly corrected her senior.

Patch saluted her playfully and added, "You know your dates. I'll bow to your wisdom." He smiled at her. "Read something from your Emerson book." He said, then added, as she opened the dark brown colored book, "I remember one quote from Emerson, 'Do not follow where the path may lead. Go instead where there is no path and leave a trail.'"

Abby smiled at Patch and opened the back of the book and began to read. "One of Emerson's major themes is his tribute to nature, like his famous poems: 'The Snow Storm 'or 'The Titmouse' or 'The Rhodora'. In fact, many have likened Emerson's 'The Humble Bee 'to Poe's 'The Raven.'" She turned to the Table of Contents for a moment. Then, she leafed through the book until she found the page she was looking for and read, "'The Humble Bee', - Burly, dozing humble-bee, / Where thou art is clime for me. / Let them sail for Porto Rique, / Far-off heats through seas to seek; / I will follow thee alone, / Thou animated torrid-zone! / Zigzag steerer, desert cheerer, / Let me chase thy waving lines; / Keep me nearer, me thy hearer, / Singing over shrubs and vines. "

"Insect lover of the sun, / Joy of thy dominion! / Sailor of the atmosphere; / Swimmer through the waves of air; / Voyager of light and noon; / Epicurean of June; / Wait, I prithee, till I come / Within earshot of thy hum, - / All without is martyrdom."

She stopped and turned to Patch. "I'll bring in 'The Raven 'and see what you think." She smiled and leafed through the book again until she found the page she was looking for and said, "'The Rhodora 'is a poetic celebration of a native New England flower, whose flowers in spring pop out before its leaves do, leaving a bouquet of purple flowers and sticks. But Emerson tells us that the flower's 'Beauty is its own excuse for being.'" She cleared her throat and read, "'The Rhodora '- On being asked, Whence is the flower? / In May, when sea-winds pierced our solitudes, / I found the fresh Rhodora in the woods, / Spreading its leafless blooms in a damp nook, / To please the desert and the sluggish brook. / The purple petals, fallen in the pool, / Made the black water with their beauty gay; / Here might the red-bird come his plumes to cool, / And court the flower that cheapens his array. / Rhodora! if the sages ask thee why / This charm is wasted on the earth and sky, / Tell them, dear, that if eyes were made for seeing, / Then Beauty is its own excuse for being: / Why thou wert there, O rival of the rose! / I never thought to ask, I never knew: / But, in my simple ignorance, suppose / The self-same Power that brought me there brought you."

She fanned herself for a moment then said, "So beautiful. Poetry like that causes you to stop and look at things that you normally just walk by and don't see." She fanned herself again and added softly, "So beautiful."

Doctor Dudley had come into the tent about half way through the poem and was checking Hunter's pulse. "That certainly was beautiful, Abby. I'm proud to see Hunter is receiving such good care." He looked over at Peg and added, "Did you know, when Emerson's protégée Henry David Thoreau died of tuberculosis at the age of 44, Emerson delivered his eulogy. And that Emerson served as one of the pallbearers when another friend, Nathaniel Hawthorne, died two years later?"

"Who's Henry David Thoreau?" Peg asked, perplexed, turning to Abby.

"Mr. Emerson was Henry David Thoreau's friend and chief mentor. In 1845, Thoreau at 28, built himself a small cabin on the shore of Walden Pond, near Concord, and for 2 years lived a solitary life, living off the land, observing nature and writing *Walden*, a book about shunning materialistic pursuits."

"'A man is rich in proportion to the number of things he can afford to leave alone.'" Doctor Dudley quoted, then added, "'The mass of men lead lives of quiet desperation.'" He smiled at Abby.

"Did you know that one of Thoreau's most important works, the essay 'Civil Disobedience', grew out of an overnight stay he did in the town's jail as a result of his conscientious refusal to pay a poll tax that supported the Mexican War, which to Thoreau represented an effort to extend slavery?"

"The Mexican American War," Peg piped up loudly. "I know the answer to that one. I was in that war." Peg scratched his face and continued. "President Polk was worried that France or Great Britain was going to buy California from the Mexicans so he sent John Slidell to Mexico to negotiate a settlement. Slidell was authorized to purchase California and New Mexico. To make a long story short, Great Britain backed away, but France wanted to close the deal under the table. So that which could not be achieved by diplomacy was achieved by all out war." Peg scratched his beard and added, "If we had not won the war, the people in California would be talking French right now instead of American."

"You mean English," Patch corrected.

"Whatever." Peg snorted and looked away.

Just then, a black orderly leaned his head around the tent door and cleared his throat, "Miss Abby, your momma is wait'n for you's in her carriage."

Abby jumped up and patted Hunter on his sleeping forehead. "I'll see you boys later," she said over her shoulder as she disappeared out the tent door.

"The Mexicans call it 'Intervención Estadounidense en México' or 'U.S. intervention in Mexico.'" Patch said to Peg as he picked up the newspaper and started absently looking through it.

"They can call it anything they want to." Peg pushed confidently back in his chair, "I call it a done deal." He sniffed loudly, spit a stream of brown juice into the brass spittoon and wiped his mouth with the sleeve of his shirt.

"Well, it was certainly that. Under the Treaty of Guadalupe Hidalgo, we not only got California and New Mexico but Mexico finally agreed to the loss of Texas and the Rio Grande River as a boundary between the two countries."

Peg, busy picking imaginary lint off his old dusty hat, sniffed. "Done deal, like I said."

"Here's an interesting headline," Patch said, changing the subject and holding up the newspaper for Peg to see. "All it says is HELENA. It seems that Helena has been a thorn in the side of the Confederacy ever since it was taken over by the Union Army. It's 70 miles downriver from Memphis, 230 miles above Vicksburg and less than 90 miles from Little Rock. And as such is a constant threat to our capital, Little Rock." Patch took a sip of coffee and continued, "It seems General Price, Old Pap as he is known by his troops, is loved by his troops but snubbed by our President Davis."

"Why?"

"It says here he argued and disagreed with the President too much."

"That will do it." Peg rubbed his beard furiously while getting ready to say more. "One time, back during the Mexican-American War, I had a Sergeant Major who…."

 "Peg," Patch snapped. "Hunter, don't care about your Mexican-American War stories, so will you please let me continue with this article?" Patch looked at Peg for a long second then continued, "Old Pap convinced Granny Holmes that their Little Rock operation would be much safer if they captured Helena. Once established there, the Rebels could harass Yankee shipping up and down the Mississippi River and maybe prevent further troop movement on the beleaguered and war weary Vicksburg." Patch read for a moment and said, "Yankees already occupied Arkansas Post, 120 miles down the Arkansas River from Little Rock, so capturing Helena and having a Rebel presence on the Mississippi sounded like a good idea to the Confederate commanders at the Trans-Mississippi Department at Shreveport, Louisiana."

"Sounds like a good idea to me, too." Patch straightened his hat and pushed himself back in his chair confidently.

"It says here that before the war Helena had a population of only 1,024 white citizens and 527 black slaves. Hum." Patch paused for a moment. "Under the Yankee General Curtis 'command, the population has grown to 20,000 troops and thousands of freed slaves."

"Don't tell me. I see it coming." Peg scrunched up his face in mock pain.
"Yep. About 300 former slaves formed three companies and were dubbed the 'First Arkansas Volunteer Infantry Regiment (African Descent)'. Their Captain Miller even wrote them a marching song that was soon adopted by other black regiments."

"I guess we're lucky there were no Indians in Helena, or they would have put them in Yankee uniforms, too," Peg said huffing and puffing.

"Frankly, we got even luckier. Just about the time Marmaduke's and Price's men were leaving Jacksonport and Holmes 'men, commanded by General Fagan, were leaving Little Rock - all headed to Helena - General Grant turns around and pulls most of the Yankee troops out of Helena to support his siege on Vicksburg."

Peg slapped his good knee and yelped, "Finally, some good luck coming our way."

"Hold on a second. That's the good news. The bad news is that Helena, being at the end of Crowley's Ridge, is in a semi-circle of hills and valleys facing the Mississippi River. And the Yankee

General Prentiss, who had survived the 'Hornets 'Nest 'at Shiloh, was not going to be caught off guard. Even though he only had 4,000 men left to defend the city, he wisely fortified the hills that wrapped around the port town with four artillery batteries. Battery A and B were on Righton Hill to the north, Battery D was on Hindman Hill to the south and Battery C was on Graveyard Hill in the middle. Now, with cannons strategically positioned on these four hilltops, all pointed toward the valleys, he had his men strew the valley floors with felled trees. Prentiss was confident that this mess of tangled trees and stumps would slow down and confuse any would-be attackers, while making their stalled and hampered efforts more vulnerable to his cannons and his sharpshooters."

Patch sipped his coffee and continued, "At first light more than 7,000 Rebels attacked the fortified city. Marmaduke attacked the hill in the north, and Fagan attacked the hill in the south. But because Price thought the order to attack was sun up, he waited an hour before attacking. During that hour, Fagan's troops got broadsided by Battery C from the hill in the middle - the one Price was supposed to have attacked at first light. Meanwhile, up in the north, Marmaduke's unprotected right flank was being mauled because our General Walker, who was assigned to protect that flank, was no place to be found." Patch sipped more coffee and added, "Finally, Price shows up. He quickly captures the hill in the middle, while taking heavy casualties, and quickly silences the killer Battery C cannons. Once the hilltop was under control, our General Homes marched in but issued a number of confusing orders that got additional soldiers killed. In the meantime, Batteries A and B and D were firing at will. The timber-clad USS Tyler was sitting in the middle of the Mississippi River lobbing shells over the Yankee's heads and destroying the Rebel soldiers trying to climb over fallen trees and make it up the sides of the different hills. It says here that Ensign George L. Smith on the USS Tyler reported firing 413 rounds, mostly eight-inch exploding shells with ten- and fifteen-second fuses."

(Dream)

With every beat of the soldier's heart, a spurt of blood leaped out from his leg. Hunter kneeled down in the dirt next to the fallen soldier and looked around frantically for help. Everyone was busy dodging bullets and ducking exploding shells. A sharp scream of pain from the fallen soldier brought Hunter's attention back from looking hopelessly for help. Another spurt of blood leaped out from his leg and another and another. Hunter ripped open the man's pants leg and saw the small hole that was causing all the spurting. Before another spurt of blood could leap out, Hunter jammed his finger deep into the hole, and the bleeding instantly stopped. He spun around on his knees looking for something to make a tourniquet out of. An officer's horse was nervously shifting from foot to foot not knowing what to do next, now that his master lay dead in the dirt. Hunter grabbed one end of the long leather reins and wrapped it a half-dozen times tightly around the man's leg, just above where his finger had stopped the bleeding. He took his finger out. No bleeding. He gasped a deep satisfying breath and sank back on his haunches in the dirt. Suddenly, the man moaned, and Hunter, still on his knees, scrambled up to the man's face and leaned down. "What's your name?" Hunter screamed trying to be heard over the shooting and shouting.

The Yankee soldier licked his dry lips and said, "Minos Miller."

"What happened?" Hunter asked, not knowing what else to say.

"We were looking drown the hill when directly we heard the Rebels cheering and knew they were charging on the batteries. In a minute we could see column after column of Rebels pouring over the hills toward Battery C. As soon as they came into sight, the gunboat and every battery that could get range of them let into them with a vengeance. The air was full of shells, and we could see the Rebel's lines open and see them falling in all directions.'"

(Hospital)

"Read that again," Peg insisted.

"It is estimated that for every one Yankee casualty, seven Rebels died at the Battle of Helena. The numbers are 239 (US) versus 1,614 (CS) casualties."

"Wow."

The timber-clad USS Tyler

"Are you ready for another wow?" Patch looked sideways at Peg and continued, "The Second Arkansas Infantry (African Descent) held the extreme left of the Union line. Although these troops were not directly attacked and suffered only five wounded, the role they played in the battle received wide notice in the Northern abolitionist press." Patch waited for Peg to say something but finally added, "By 10:30 that morning, General Homes issued the order to retreat. The short Battle of Helena was over."

"Black soldiers, fallen trees, cannons all over the hill tops, gunboats with exploding shells and ten- and fifteen-second fuses, can it get any worse?"

Running Vicksburg Blockade

"Yep. Get this. General Walker, who was supposed to have protected Marmaduke's left flank, was too busy protecting his own left flank and never came to Marmaduke's aid. Outraged that his men got mauled by small arms fire, Marmaduke, after the retreat, went looking for Walker ready to 'run him through' with his saber."

"Great. Now we've got generals trying to kill generals. As if the Yankees needed any more help," Peg snorted and rubbed his beard furiously.

Patch read for a moment then added, "The Rebel's defeat at Helena was further marred by the news that Vicksburg had fallen to the Yankees the very same day. Then, to add salt to insult, they got news that just the day before General Lee had lost at Gettysburg."

They sat in silence for a long while. Peg had taken off his hat and was fussing with the dust on the brim while Patch looked blankly at the folded newspaper in his lap.

CHAPTER 9 - DEVIL'S BACKBONE & YANKEES IN THE CAPITAL

(Hospital)

Abby picked up a book from her lap and said, "Nathaniel Hawthorne." She opened it up and read, "Nathaniel Hawthorne was fascinated by the dark side of the Puritan mind. One of his ancestors was a judge in the Salem Witch Trials during 1692 and 1693. His novels, especially *The Scarlet Letter* (1850) and *The House of Seven Gables* (1851), deal with revenge, guilt, and pride."

"Wow, that is pretty heavy stuff for a sleeping boy," Patch offered.

"I know. I know," Abby agreed. "Oh, it says here that when Nathaniel Hawthorne died at the age of 60, Ralph Waldo Emerson and Longfellow were among his pallbearers and that Longfellow wrote 'The Bells of Lynn 'as a tribute poem to his close friend." She put the Hawthorne book down and searched in her lap for a second. "Here is a book by Henry Wadsworth Longfellow." She opened it up and read to herself for a moment and then said, "Oh, I love this poem that tells about Paul Revere's midnight ride to warn the Minutemen during the American Revolution that the British were coming." She cleared her throat and read, "Listen my children and you shall hear / Of the midnight ride of Paul Revere, / On the eighteenth of April, in Seventy-five; / Hardly a man is now alive / Who remembers that famous day and year. / He said to his friend, "If the British march / By land or sea from the town to-night, / Hang a lantern aloft in the belfry arch / Of the North Church tower as a signal light,-- / One if by land, and two if by sea; / And I on the opposite shore will be, / Ready to ride and spread the alarm / Through every Middlesex village and farm, / For the country folk to be up and to arm."

She laid the book down in her lap and closed her eyes for a second. "Now, that is powerful storytelling poetry." She opened to the back of the book and read quietly for a second, "It says here that the poems that made Longfellow a household name were 'The Song of Hiawatha '(1855), 'The Courtship of Miles Standish '(1858), 'Tales of a Wayside Inn', and especially 'Evangeline 'and 'A Tale of Acadie '(1847)." She paused for a second and looked at Patch. "I didn't know this." She read on. "In 1713, the British gained control of Nova Scotia, the home to thousands of French-speaking farmers and fishermen known as Acadians. British officials harbored doubts about the Acadians' loyalties and settled upon a policy of forced relocation for those unwilling to take an oath of loyalty to the British crown and renounce Catholicism."

"Catholicism," Patch interjected, "had been banned from England ever since 1533 when the Pope would not grant Henry the Eighth an annulment of marriage from his first wife Catherine of Aragon, because she had not bore him a male child and an heir to the royal throne."

"Correct." Abby smiled at Patch. "That's what it says right here. Those who would not renounce Catholicism and join the Church of England were uprooted, and the bulk of their personal property was destroyed or left behind. One group of Acadian refugees settled in Louisiana, an area with a strong French influence and a Roman Catholic majority. These newcomers became known as the 'Cajuns, 'a corruption of the French word Acadians. This event was memorialized in Longfellow's poem 'Evangeline.'"

"Wow, that sounds like the Trail of Tears," Peg scoffed. "I guess if you can't beat'm, move'm."

"Peg, will you give it a rest?" Patch turned to Abby, "You said that

Longfellow wrote 'The Bells of Lynn 'as a tribute poem to his dead friend Hawthorne."

"Yes." And she turned to a new page in the book and read, "HEARD AT NAHANT. Nahant is where Longfellow lived." She cleared her throat and read, "HEARD AT NAHANT - O curfew of the setting sun! O Bells of Lynn! / O requiem of the dying day! O Bells of Lynn! / From the dark belfries of yon cloud-cathedral wafted, / Your sounds aerial seem to float, O Bells of Lynn! / Borne on the evening wind across the crimson twilight, / O'er land and sea they rise and fall, O Bells of Lynn! / The fisherman in his boat, far out beyond the headland, / Listens, and leisurely rows ashore, O Bells of Lynn! / Over the shining sands the wandering cattle homeward / Follow each other at your call, O Bells of Lynn! / The distant lighthouse hears, and with his flaming signal / Answers you, passing the watchword on, O Bells of Lynn! / And down the darkening coast run the tumultuous surges, / And clap their hands, and shout to you, O Bells of Lynn! / Till from the shuddering sea, with your wild incantations, / Ye summon up the spectral moon, O Bells of Lynn! / And startled at the sight like the weird woman of Endor, / Ye cry aloud, and then are still, O Bells of Lynn!"

Just then, a black orderly leaned his head around the tent door and cleared his throat, "Miss Abby, your momma is wait'n for you's in her carriage."

Abby jumped up and patted Hunter on his sleeping forehead. "I'll see you boys later," she said over her shoulder as she disappeared out the tent door.

Peg watched as Abby disappeared out the tent door. He turned to Patch and sniffed. "If you ask me that 'O Bells of Lynn 'wasn't all that giggly either." Peg spit a stream of brown juice into the brass spittoon and wiped his mouth with the sleeve of his shirt. "Maybe we should of stuck with Nathaniel Hawthorne and his fascination with the dark side of the Puritan mind."

"Give Longfellow a break. That was an ode to Hawthorne, a fallen friend." Patch touched his cheek thoughtfully for a second. Then, he recited from memory. "'I shot an arrow into the air, / It fell to earth, I knew not where; / For, so swiftly it flew, the sight / Could not follow it in its flight. 'Henry Wadsworth Longfellow's The Arrow and the Song." Patch bowed a little in his chair.

"Give me a break," Peg snorted. "Can we get back to the battlefield newspaper?"

Patch picked up the newspaper from his lap and read to himself for a moment and then said, "Oh, look. The old Fort Gibson in Indian Territory has been renamed to Fort Blunt."

"Who's the general in charge, General Blunt?" Peg said, looking sideways at Patch.

"Yep."

"Wow, go figure."

"It looks like the Yankees have moved out into Indian Territory. General Blunt jumped our General Steele at Honey Springs and scattered 6,500 Rebel troops, who tried to fight the best they could with defective gun powder." Patch paused then added, "It says the Battle of Honey Springs was unique in the fact that white soldiers were the minority in both forces. Indians and blacks made up significant portions of each of the opposing armies."

Peg rolled his eyes back into his head and slid silently back into his chair.

Fort Smith Court House

Patch didn't bother to look over at Peg; he just continued. "It looks like another one of our generals, General Cabell, was holding down the fort at Fort Smith, Arkansas, when he got news that General Blunt with 4,500 freshly reinforced and re-supplied Yankee troops were moving out of Indian Territory to attack Fort Smith and that additional Yankees were coming down from Springfield, Missouri, to help." Patch took a sip of his coffee and continued, "It says General Cabell loaded up his wagons and moved them 10 miles south to Old Jenny Lind but paused there only briefly. His goal was to get the wagons over a ridge called Devil's Backbone and on down to the safety of Waldron, Arkansas, 40 miles to the south."

"Devil's Backbone, that sounds nasty." Peg declared.

"It got nasty for the Rebels. It says here that Blunt took Fort Smith without opposition and sent his General Cloud after Cabell. Our General Cabell ambushed and momentarily halted his pursuers at the base of the Devil's Backbone. However, under the cover of artillery fire, Cloud regrouped his men, formed a line of dismounted cavalry with howitzers and attacked. With the Kansas cavalry on their left, the Missouri cavalry on their right and Union artillery coming up the middle firing canisters that tore into their ranks, the Southerners slowly but steadily fell back from their ambush position. The battle lasted three hours, enough time for Cabell to get his supply wagons over Devil's Backbone and toward safety. Once he did, he fell back and the Yankees claimed victory."

"Victory?" Peg huffed. "After three hours?" Peg huffed again. "It was a hard won victory, at best, because our boys sure didn't give it away." He spit a stream of brown juice into the brass spittoon and wiped his mouth with the sleeve of his shirt. "I hope the Yankees enjoy their new summer home at Fort Smith. It didn't cost General Blunt anything to move in."

"It says here Blunt didn't enjoy it. His troops and supply lines were constantly harassed by Indian soldiers under General Watie and by so called Partisan Rangers also known as Bushwhackers."

"Good," Peg huffed to himself and then began to whine. "Man, can you believe it? The Yankees now own both ends of the Arkansas River. Now, they've got troops at Fort Smith to add to the troops they have at Arkansas Post, at the other end of the Arkansas River." Peg absently picked imaginary lint off his old dusty hat and added, "Well, at least we still own Little Rock, right smack-dab in the middle."

"Not according to this article." Patch sipped more coffee and quipped, "The editor of the 'Arkansas Patriot 'wrote this, 'Any head with a thimble full of brains ought to know the fate of Arkansas rest intimately upon the fate of Vicksburg.'"

"Balderdash," Peg declared.

"Not so, my fine feathered friend. It says here that General Grant's victory at Vicksburg freed up thousands of Yankee troops and gunboats that could now move freely up and down the Mighty Mississip." Patch sipped his coffee and added, "It says here that General Grant was advised by his staff that owning the Arkansas River would command a strong hold on the state and prevent any further attacks into Missouri from northern Arkansas." He paused then concluded, "Owning the river includes owning Little Rock."

"You're kidding."

"Nope. In fact, General Grant dispatched General Steele from Helena with that goal in mind."

(Dream)

General Steele shook the officer's hand with a firm handshake. "That's a pretty strong handshake you have there, young man," General Steel said, taking a cigar from Hunter's hand and handing it to the officer. "Hunter, pour General Davidson some sherry." The General handed the reins of his horse to an officer next to him. "I'm sorry I'm late. How long have you been waiting in this God forsaken swamp?"

"We came down the Old Military Road atop Crowley's Ridge from Missouri and have been here now about 10 days." He took the sherry from Hunter and leaned down to let him light his cigar. "I'm sorry to say that we started off with 6,000 cavalry soldiers, but we've lost over 1,000 of them already."

General Steele sipped his sherry and looked at the office over the top of his glass. "I'm sorry to hear that causality counts. Are the Rebels that thick around here?"

"No, they are not dead, sir," General Davidson said. "It's the malaria and fever that has made them sick and not able to stand muster. As for the Rebel resistance, it is mostly small arms fire from Partisans Rangers."

"Are 1,000 sick? Well, there is a simple solution to that." General Steele turned to Hunter. "Hunter, go spread the word that we are leaving Clarendon immediately and headed up the White River to De Valls Bluff." He turned to General Davidson and patted him on the back as they walked along the riverbank. "De Valls Bluff is higher ground and not as swampy as Clarendon is." They both laughed. "Say, I understand you're a West Pointer and passed up a commission by the CSA to join the USA. Why?" General Steele asked.

"I was born and raised in Virginia. As you know, even though the eastern side of Virginia was settled rapidly, the western side with its rugged terrain restricted any quick migration. However, after the American Revolution, largely non-slave owning settlers moved into western Virginia. With the outbreak of the Civil War, residents from western Virginia voted against the ordinance of secession in 1861. In 1863, West Virginia was admitted to the Union as the 35th state." General Davidson stopped walking and turned to General Steele. "I guess I just went along with my family, friends and neighbors and stayed with the Union."

"Ah, the CSA's loss and our gain." General Steele clinked his glass to General Davidson's, puffed deeply on his cigar and smiled.

(Hospital)

"Read that again," Peg requested.

"It says here General Steel combined his men with General Davidson's men and took command of the 12,000 Yankees and started moving them toward the capital"

"What was Little Rock doing about it?"

Patch read quietly to himself for a moment and then answered. "General Homes, Granny, had fallen ill after losing at Helena, and General Price had taken over command of the troops. Unfortunately, there were not that many troops to command, only 8,000 with no hope of receiving any more from the central command."

"Why?

"Now, get this. General Kirby-Smith, the Confederate commander of the Trans-Mississippi Department in Shreveport, Louisiana, had written off the whole state of Arkansas and had moved the Confederacy's new Trans-Mississippi line of defense down to the Red River."

"The Red River? Where's that?"

"The Red River flows from up in the northwestern tip of Texas all the way down through Indian Territory, Arkansas and Louisiana before it empties into the Gulf of Mexico. In fact, it is the natural northern boundary between Texas and Indian Territory, and it's the natural northeastern boundary between Texas and Arkansas."

"So Kirby-Smith wrote off Arkansas?" Peg mumbled under his breath.

Patch didn't look at Peg but said, "Well, the Confederate's Trans-Mississippi Department may have given up on Arkansas, but the

Yankees sure haven't. From this article, it looks like they are looking forward to moving into the state's capital. It says here that General Steele with 12,000 men and 57 cannons left De Valls Bluff in a hurry, headed straight for Little Rock, only 50 short miles away."

"Wow, 12,000 Yankees packing 57 cannons," Peg mumbled. "I bet Little Rock was not too happy with that little bit of news."

"Nope. Little Rock started emptying out immediately. The new Confederate Governor Flanagin packed up and moved the capital 100 miles southwest to a small town called Washington." Patch read for a moment then added, "Get this. Price ordered Marmaduke to join forces with General Walker to cover and protect the relocation activity. And since Walker was the superior officer, he was put in charge of the overall activities."

"Is this the same Walker that let Marmaduke's troops get mauled at Helena and the same Walker who Marmaduke, after the retreat, went looking for, ready to 'run him through 'with his saber?"

"Yep."

"What was General Price thinking putting Walker over Marmaduke and his troops?" Peg looked sideways at Patch and added. "That all happened less than, what?"

"Less than two months ago." Patch helped with the calculation and then added, "I don't know what Price was thinking; nonetheless, he sent both of them together to Lonoke, about halfway between Little Rock and De Valls Bluff, to wait for the approaching Yankees." Patch sipped his coffee and continued, "They didn't have to wait long. Marmaduke's 1,300 horsemen were soon outnumbered and hit hard by four times more Yankees with eight times more artillery. Marmaduke fought hard as he slowly pulled back to Reed's Bridge on Bayou Meto, about 12 miles northeast of downtown Little Rock. By noon the next day, the troops were in position, and the fight was on again. The Yankees, under Davidson's command, fought their way down to the bridge. But before they could cross it, the Rebels set it on fire. The fighting was hot and heavy until nightfall."

"I don't care how many Yanks they throw at us. Our boys are going to hold them at the bridge," Peg snorted and pushed himself defiantly back into his chair.

"That night, the Rebels pulled back from the bridge to within 5 miles of Little Rock and the Arkansas River. There they dug in and waited. But it seems Steele was not in a hurry to attack Little Rock. He would take a couple of days to put together an attack plan while his troops bivouacked with Davidson's troops. The 10,477 men, present for duty, leisurely waited for fresh supplies, ammunition and provisions to be brought up from De Valls Bluff."

"Man, 10,477 Yankees perched on the other side of the Arkansas River." Peg leaned slightly forwards. "I wonder what the Rebel generals thought about all that?"

"One was dead."

"Whatch-u-talkin-bout Patch?" Peg scrunched up his face and fish-eyed Patch sideways.

"Marmaduke killed Walker." Patch stared back at Peg and then added, "Killed him in a duel."

(Dream)

"General, I don't want to say it," Hunter pleaded.

"Say it." The General snarled.

"General, I really don't want to do this." Hunter paused then leaned in a little and with a lowered voice added, "You see I've got the measles and have been..."

"Shut up," the general snarled. "Say it Hunter, or I'll knock you down."

Hunter nervously cocked the hammer of the Colt Navy revolver and handed it to the general.

"Now, say it," the general insisted.

"General, I've been kicked in the head...."

The general pointed the revolver at Hunter and snarled, "Hunter!"

"Gentlemen, are you ready?" Hunter squealed quickly.

Both duelists answered, "Yes."

Hunter nervously cleared his throat, and then in a pinched but clear voice hollered loudly, "Ready, one, two, three — fire."

(Hospital)

"Read that again," Peg insisted.

Patch sipped his coffee. "The duel took place at dawn at the Godfrey-LeFevre place, seven miles below little Rock on the north side of the Arkansas River. It seems during the fight at Reed's Bridge Marmaduke had requested several times during the day that General Walker, his superior officer, join him on the front lines to confer on strategy against the attacking Northerners. Walker refused to leave his headquarters at the rear of the Confederate lines. Later, when Marmaduke loudly questioned Walker's bravery and asked that he either be released from Walker's command or that his resignation be accepted, Walker demanded 'satisfaction,' or challenged Marmaduke to a duel.

"The duelists agreed to face each other at sunrise armed with Colt Navy revolvers at fifteen paces. The weapons were to be placed in the hands of the two generals cocked and held at a 45-degree angle. When the word was given, 'Gentlemen, are you ready? 'If both answered 'yes, 'then the call would be: 'Ready, one, two, three — fire. 'After that, both men would shoot at will without leaving their places until all bullets were fired or one of the men fell.

"Walker arrived with his friends at the site one hour before daybreak, while Marmaduke and his supporters came just at dawn. As soon as there was enough light, a friend of each man measured the field and marked the duelists 'places with chunks of wood. The field was lined up north and south so that neither man would get an advantage from the rising sun.

"The two men took their positions, and when the word was given, both fired simultaneously. Neither was hurt. After a short pause, Marmaduke shot a second time. The ball struck Walker in the side, passing through the right kidney and lodging in the spine causing paralysis of his legs. Marmaduke offered the use of his ambulance to transport the mortally wounded Walker back to Little Rock, which was gratefully accepted. Arriving at about 10 a.m., Walker and his friends stopped at the home of Mrs. Cates, where the general died the next evening."

"Great!" Peg hooted and stomped his wooden leg. "As if the Yankees aren't killing enough of our men, Marmaduke has to lend them a helping hand." Peg stomped his wooden leg again and looked unblinkingly at Patch. "I'm serious. I think they should arrest Marmaduke for destroying government property and hampering the war effort." Peg rubbed his beard furiously in disbelief and added angrily, "Maybe they should go hang him for helping and abetting the enemy." Peg spit a stream of brown juice into the brass spittoon and angrily wiped his mouth with the sleeve of his shirt. "What the heck was Price doing all this time?"

"Well, our General Price had his hands full. It says he had told both generals to stay in their quarters and not leave them for any reason."

"Humph, that order was followed to a T," Peg groused.

"General Price knew he was facing an impending invasion, so he issued a request to the citizens of Little Rock to come help him fight the Yankees or be overrun." Patch read to himself for a moment then added, "Now get this, '... or be over run by a merciless and vindictive foe, and either be driven with your wives and daughters into a homeless exile or be forced to crouch in servile and degrading submission at the feet of the conquerors.'"

"Did the call to action work?"

"I don't think so."

(Dream)

General Steele handed Hunter the reins to his horse and moved in closer to the circle of officers that had been standing waiting for his arrival.

"You two." He pointed at two officers. "You two, tomorrow morning you take a diversionary force a little ways up the river and threaten Buck's Ford. Make a lot of noise going up there, and press the attack seriously as if this is where we plan to cross the Arkansas River." He paused and looked around at the faces. "You six. A little south of here the river makes almost an S curve. I want your people to go down there right now, and during the night, build me a pontoon bridge strong enough to support the passage of infantry and cavalry horses. And don't make any noise doing it." He paused again and looked around at the faces. "You four. I want eight cannons on both shoulders of the S curve, pointed across the river, so that when the Rebels move up their cannons to stop us from building the bridge and crossing it, you will have them in crossfire. Make it so hot for them that... that... that..." The general stopped and looked around. "Hunter!" The general pulled Hunter closer into the circle of officers. "Measles boy, now what's the word I'm looking for? Make it so hot...

what?"

Hunter looked over his right shoulder, then over his left shoulder, as if the general was talking to a Hunter standing behind him. "I.... I.... I don't know, sir." Hunter stammered nervously. "I.... I.... I'm sorry. Sir. I wasn't listening." Hunter stammered even more nervously. "I.... I.... I was just standing here holding the horses...."

"That's it." The general turned to his four artillery commanders and ordered, "Make it so hot with your cannonading that the Rebels will want to get on their horses and get out of town." The circle of officers broke into uproarious laughter, as the general playfully slapped Hunter on the back and held up his right hand in victory.

(Hospital)

"It says here that the Yankee general Steele had Davidson build pontoon bridges and put them down river to attack Little Rock from the south. His sixteen cannons made short work of the four Rebel cannons sent to prevent the Yankees from crossing the river. Steele hoped his rear-flanking action would cause the Rebels to re-think their defensive position north of him on the east side of the river. And it did. The Rebels got word that Yankees were preparing to come in from behind them on the other side of the river, so they quickly pulled back across the river and repositioned themselves in the streets of Little Rock, the streets from which the citizens of the town had totally and completely vacated."

"So much for the call to action," Peg huffed. "I guess instead of standing and fighting, the citizens of Little Rock would rather 'crouch in servile submission.'" Peg spit a stream of brown juice into the brass spittoon and added in disgust, "It sounds to me as if the Yankees just walked right into the capital."

"Not. Marmaduke and his cavalry hit Davidson's men head-on a few miles from where the Yankees swarmed across their pontoon bridge, at a little stream called Fourche Bayou. It says here that 'a heavy crossfire of grape, canister, and spherical case plus fierce Rebel resistance stopped Davidson dead in his tracks.'" Patch paused and added, "In Davidson's report he wrote, 'every foot of ground from this point onward was warmly contested by the Rebels.'"

Peg cleared his throat and pushed back into his chair confidently. "I guess our Mr. Marmaduke showed their Mr. Davidson our boys can't be pushed around 'by a merciless and vindictive foe.'"

The Old State House - Little Rock

"Well, they can be if they get pummeled from across the river from Steele's cannons. It says here that once Steele's gunners got the range they hammered the Rebel position unmercifully until they gave up the cornfield and fell back, but fell back begrudgingly." Patch sipped his coffee and continued, "Marmaduke got word that our General Price's army was leaving town and was headed 60 miles south to Arkadelphia to re-group. Marmaduke's cavalry reluctantly joined the evacuation."

"So the Yankees now own Little Rock."

"And the Arsenal. Remember the Union Arsenal a few years back that started and ended the Civil War in Arkansas, on the same day?"

"And the victorious parades down the Arkansas River from Fort Smith." Peg rubbed his beard furiously.

"Well, the Yankees swept in so quickly that they captured the Arsenal before it could be put to fire and captured, in the process, 3,000 pounds of powder and a considerable quantity of cartridges." Patch read quietly to himself for a moment and then added, "I guess their General Steele feels that the war was over, too. He wrote this to his Yankee superiors in Washington D.C., 'From all accounts, Price's Confederate army is demoralized and half disbanded. I am told they have made preliminary arrangements to move further south into Texas. I am satisfied that the majority of the citizens of the state of Arkansas are tired of the Rebel oppression and earnestly desire the re-establishment of the old United States Government.'"

"Tired of Rebel oppression?" Peg scrunched up his face and fish-eyed Patch sideways "Does that pickled-headed-goose realize that THEY, the Yankees, are the oppressors? That THEY, the Yankees, are the invaders? That THEY sweep down out of the north, like hungry swarms of locusts, and invaded OUR country, the Confederate States of America? That THEY are oppressing our people and our Southern way of life with their foreign rules and regulations?"

Little Rock Arsenal

CHAPTER 10 - PINE BLUFF & HANGED AT 17

(Hospital)

Abby sat next to Hunter's cot with a book in her lap and a smile on her face. She cleared her throat and read the introduction out loud. "John Greenleaf Whittier was born December 17, 1807, in Haverhill, Massachusetts, the son of two devout Quakers. He worked passionately for a series of abolitionist newspapers and magazines and was good friends with Ralph Waldo Emerson, Henry Wadsworth Longfellow, Oliver Wendell Holmes and Mark Twain. An event during the Civil War inspired his famous poem, 'Barbara Frietchie.' According to the story, at the age of 90, Miss Frietchie waved the Union flag in the middle of the street to block, or at least antagonize Stonewall Jackson's troops, as they passed through her town of Frederick during their Maryland Campaign. This event is the subject of John Greenleaf Whittier's poem 'Barbara Frietchie.'" Abby cleared her throat again and read, "'Shoot, if you must, this old gray head, / But spare your country's flag," she said. / A shade of sadness, a blush of shame, / Over the face of the leader came; / The nobler nature within him stirred / To life at that woman's deed and word; / "Who touches a hair of yon gray head / Dies like a dog! March on!" he said.'"

"And that's right, 'The nobler nature within him stirred.'" Peg turned and pointed a finger at Patch. "And that, good buddy, is the kind of Southern gentleman General Stonewall Jackson was." Peg cleared the lump in his throat and continued in a deeper voice. "It's a shame his own men shot him. He could of done so much for the cause."

"Wait. It must be his birthday or something because there is a short biography here in the back of one of these newspapers." Patch leafed through the three or four newspapers stacked in his lap until he found the one he was looking for. "Here it is." He turned to the back of the paper and started to read, "Thomas Jonathan 'Stonewall 'Jackson, born January 21, 1824, died May 10, 1863, was probably the most well-known Confederate commander after General Robert E. Lee. His military career includes the Valley Campaign of 1862 and his service as a corps commander in the Army of Northern Virginia under Robert E. Lee. Confederate pickets accidentally shot him at the Battle of Chancellorsville on May 2, 1863, which the general survived, albeit with the loss of an arm to amputation. However, he died of complications of pneumonia eight days later. His death was a severe setback for the Confederacy, affecting not only its military prospects, but also the morale of its army and of the general public."

"I still can't believe his own men shot him," Peg gasped.

Patch ignored his comment and continued to read, "Military historians consider Jackson to be one of the most gifted tactical commanders in United States history. His Valley Campaign and his envelopment of the Union Army right wing at Chancellorsville are still studied as examples of innovative and bold leadership. He excelled as well in other battles: the First Battle of Bull Run - where he received his famous nickname 'Stonewall '- the Second Battle of Bull Run, Antietam, and Fredericksburg."

Just then, a black orderly leaned his head around the tent door and cleared his throat, "Miss Abby, your momma is wait'n for you's in her carriage."

Abby jumped up and patted Hunter on his sleeping forehead. "I'll see you boys later," she said over her shoulder as she disappeared out the tent door.

"I love Stonewall Jackson as much as I love and respect General

Marmaduke." Peg yawned and stretched a little. "I wonder what our boy general is doing nowadays?"

"It says here," Patch began and then tapped a paragraph in the same newspaper, "that while Price moved his Rebel army to Arkadelphia then finally to Camden, about 60 miles from the new capitol of Washington, Marmaduke was busy moving his cavalry to Princeton, about 30 miles southwest of the now Yankee controlled Pine Bluff."

Peg looked sideways at Patch and mumbled, "Yankee controlled Pine Bluff? When did that happen? I thought you said that Pine Bluff was the only port on the Arkansas River that we controlled."

"Not," Patch offered, without looking up. "Three days after they beat up our boys and moved into Little Rock, the Yankees moved 40 miles downriver to Pine Bluff and walked in without a cap being fired."

"Well, it sounds like my main man Marmaduke is getting ready to put a different spin on that cap," Peg snickered.

"Could be. The Yankees now own everything on the Arkansas River from Fort Smith to Little Rock to Pine Bluff to Arkansas Post down to the 'T 'at the Mississippi River, over 270 miles of northwest to southeast river that cuts the state mostly in half."

"Tell me that my main man Marmaduke is about to change all of that. Tell me he's getting ready to take it to the Pines," Peg pleaded.

"It looks like it. It says here his plan was to attack the Yankee held Pine Bluff with 2,000 men and 12 cannons. He was going to split his men up into three groups and attack Pine Bluff from three sides and push the Yankees back into the Arkansas River."

"Attack! That sounds like a good plan to me." Peg rubbed his good leg and did a little dance in his chair.

Patch read for a moment and continued, "Oops, it looks like one prong of the fork, as it moved around to get into position, bumped into a Yankee patrol. After some shots were fired, the Rebels, under a flag of truce, approached the Yankee Lieutenant." Patch read more then added. "The Rebels demanded passage through the Union lines to present the Yankee commander with a demand for surrender."

"Wow. That's bold."

"I guess the Yankee Lieutenant thought so, too. He drew his sidearm and huffed, 'Colonel Clayton will never surrender Pine Bluff, but he is anxious for you to come and try to take it away from him. 'With that he kicked the Rebel's horse, rode back to his men and started shooting at each other again. The Lieutenant dispatched one of his men to warn the camp commander, Colonel Clayton, and report what had happened."

"Great. So much for surprise attacks." Peg mused to himself and then added, "However, us Southerners are gentlemen, and this is suppose to be a gentlemen's war after all."

"Well then, you are not going to like this next piece of news." Patch folded the paper in his lap and continued, "When Colonel Clayton got the news, he immediately sent skirmishers out in all directions. He put 300 freed slaves to working stacking big bales of cotton all around the courthouse. He positioned his 9 cannons facing down all of the streets that led up to the courthouse and put sharpshooters in buildings all around town. Additional black freemen were put to work carrying water up from the river for a 2-day supply. It says that once the battle was on, these same freemen picked up rifles from fallen Yankee soldiers and defended an attack from the river direction."

"Blah. Blah. Blah. Just tell me that Marmaduke owns Pine Bluff."
"I can't. It says here that Marmaduke fought all day, but with his best efforts, he still could not dislodge the Yankees. It quotes him here as saying, 'They fought like devils.'"

(Dream)

Mrs. Bell grabbed Hunter by the sleeve and pulled him urgently to the side of the big window. She angrily pressed her cheek to his as they peeked around the edge of the window and watched the blue-coated officers pull their hot and wheezing animals to a grinding halt in front of the Bell house. They slid effortlessly out of their saddles and were up the front stairs, with their side arms drawn, within a heartbeat, banging noisily on the big wooden front door.

"Here, put more bandages on the children. I want those Yankee officers to believe that we're having a smallpox epidemic here in the house. This is the first brick house in the county other than the courthouse, and they'll want to use it for their headquarters. I'm not going to let those nasty foreigners disgrace my family's home like that."

Just then, the front door burst open, and the parlor was instantly filled with Yankee officers. The two young children wrapped in bandages cleaved to Mrs. Bell's dress tails, like chicks to a mother hen, and all but disappeared in her multi-layered dress. Hunter, still with a handful of white bandages, all but disappeared behind Mrs. Bell also. "What is the meaning of bursting into a private home like this?" Mrs. Bell demanded. "Can't you heathens see we have a smallpox epidemic..." But before she could finish her sentence, the whole house shook as if it was going to come off its foundation. Everyone dropped to their knees as white plaster, like snow, fell from the ceiling, blanketing the room and everyone in it with a white chalky cloud of dust.

In stunned silence, everyone stayed crouched down, not sure what just happened or what was going to happen next. Then, at the top of the steps, there was a bump and then another bump and then another bump. It was as if a giant, with shoes of lead, was at the top of the stairs, slowly clumped down one stair step at a time. Bump. Bump. Bump.

Everyone watched in shock and awe as a cannon ball bumped down to the last step and rolled across the floor and disappeared into the next room.

(Hospital)

Peg laughed and slapped his good knee. "Read that again."

"It says that Mrs. Bell, to prevent the Yankees from using her family home, wrapped up two small children in bandages and told the Yankees there was a smallpox epidemic."

"And the cannonball?"

"It says that a Union cannon located on the courthouse square fired a cannonball that went through the house and rolled across the floor."

Peg laughed and laughed until he started coughing. He spit a stream of brown juice into the brass spittoon and wiped the tears from his eyes, with the sleeve of his shirt. "That's funny. I don't care who you are. That's funny."

Patch smiled to himself as he tapped a paragraph in the paper. "It says here that since General Marmaduke was unable to take the city, he emptied it of everything that wasn't nailed down. It says he took 250 mules and horses and all the supplies he could carry. What he did not carry away he burned, like four hundred blankets and quilts and over six thousand bales of cotton. He and his troops in stolen wagons hauled their booty the 70 miles back to Camden and General Price." Patch sipped his coffee and continued, "It seems Camden and the whole southwest corner of Arkansas had become a nesting place for the Rebel army until the Trans-Mississippi Command in Louisiana decided what they wanted to do next."

"And what did they decide to do?" Peg mumbled, still wiping tears from his eyes, with the sleeve of his shirt.

"It seems while they waited for the generals in Shreveport to come up with a 'master plan', they busied themselves with harassing the Federals anywhere and everywhere they could. The two sides bumped into each other at Lunenburg, Jacksonport, Rolling Prairie, and Sylmore. And that is just to name a few of the places they skirmished." Patch paused. "The Yankee general who commanded the troops in Batesville reported killing 286 guerrillas and Confederate volunteers and capturing hundreds more."

"Man, it sounds like Johnny Reb was busy as little bees."

"Well, not only was Johnny Reb busy, but the Feds were busy, too. They held elections and elected a new Governor and enacted a new constitution, banning slavery. The new Governor, Isaac Murphy, was elected by a vote of 12,177 to 266."

"Imagine that!" Peg grumbled. "Surprise. Surprise."

"Isaac Murphy? Remember, he was the only 'no 'vote to Arkansas 'seceding from the Union and somebody tossed him a bouquet of flowers in thanks? Well, he's now Mr. Governor." Patch sipped his coffee. "It sounds like Little Rock is getting back to normal again. Businessmen are doing business as food and supplies are becoming more and more plentiful."

"Blah. Blah. Blah." Peg defiantly spit a stream of brown juice into the brass spittoon. "Isaac Murphy. I knew I didn't like him. He's probably a Yankee spy." Peg sniped. "Where's he from?"

"I don't know." Patch said looking back at the paper. "Here it is. He was born near Pittsburgh, Pennsylvania," Patch quickly added, as Peg started to swell up. "And He's a Republican."

"A Republican?" Peg scoffed. "I knew it. Lincoln is a Republican. He's a Lincoln spy. They should hang him, not make him Governor of Arkansas."

"They did."

"They hung the Governor?" Peg jerked his head around and gasped at Patch.

"No, you silly goose. They hung a spy named David O. Dodd. It seems this 17-year-old boy, David O. Dodd, was carrying a coded message about where the Federal defenses were positioned around Little Rock, and they caught him, tried him and hung him."

(Dream)

Hunter was sitting in a squeaky old wooden chair, slightly bent over watching the shadow of his boot dance back and forth in the candlelight. He was sent 20 minutes ago to light all the candles in the big dusty courtroom, and now he was waiting to be told what to do next.

He lazily leaned back in his chair, locked his fingers behind his head, yawned and sprang to his feet - all at the same time, as the doors burst open and the room was suddenly filled with Union officers and then more officers. Hunter stood at attention, not sure what else to do.
"Hunter, help the guard with the prisoner," one of the officers barked at Hunter.

Hunter rushed forward and held up one side of the frail, skinny child they had in chains and referred to as 'the prisoner'. The young fellow stumbled again and would have fallen, if it were not for Hunter's helping hand. He was dirty and disheveled and etched on his dirty young face were tear-tracks that glistened in the flickering candlelight. Thick mud was caked on the toes of his boots where he had been dragged mercilessly across the wet parade ground. The rusty iron shackles cuffed around each bony wrist had his white skin oozing blood, and he winced with pain when one of the officers pulled hard to check if they were still securely locked.

"What's your name, sir?" the officer, who barked at Hunter, asked the boy.

"David Owen Dodd, sir." The young man's voice quivered slightly as a cold shiver swept through his body.

"I'm the Judge Advocate in these proceedings, and you are being arraigned upon the following charges and specifications." The officer cleared his throat and in a lower, meaner voice, continued, "In this, that said David O. Dodd, an inhabitant of the State of Arkansas, did

as a spy of the so-called Confederate States of America, enter within the lines of the Army of the United States, stationed at Little Rock, Arkansas, and did there secretly possess himself of information regarding the number, the kind, and position of the troops of said Army of the United States, their commanders, and other military information valuable to the enemy now at war with the United States, and having thus obtained said information did obtain a pass from the Provost Marshal General's office, and endeavor to reach the lines of the enemy - therewith; when he was arrested at the cavalry outposts of said Army - and did otherwise lurk, and act as a spy of the Rebels now in arms against the United States - This at the Post of Little Rock, and the encampments of the Army of Arkansas, on or about the 29th and 30th of December, 1863." The officer slammed the paper down on the desk and glared at the young man. "How do you plead?"

"Not guilty," the young man whispered.

The officer jumped up from behind the big wooden table and leaned forwards. The veins in his neck were bulging out and throbbing, as his face turned beet red. "Louder." He screamed into the young boy's face, now only inches away. "Louder. So these men who have come to bear witness against you can hear your dirty, rotten, filthy lies." Spittle was coming out of the angry officer's mouth. "Now. Say it again, but louder."

"Not guilty," the boy squeaked, now visibly quivering as he tried to stand straight.

"Lies. Lies. Lies." The officer screamed and slammed his fist down on the wood tabletop. "And I'll prove it." The officer looked around the room. He pointed an angry and shaking finger at an enlisted man. "You there. Come forward. State your name and your business."

"My name is Sergeant Frederick Miehr of Company B, 1ˢ Missouri Cavalry." The sergeant cleared his throat and continued, "I was on picket on the Benton road about twelve miles from Little Rock. I had been on picket only a short time when my inside vedette halted a

man, and I looked up and saw the prisoner, that is I think it was him, coming into the main road. I then went to where the vedette was. I asked the prisoner if he had a pass, and he said he did not. He said he had had a pass for two days, and the picket on the Hot Spring road took it from him. I asked him where he lived and he said at Little Rock. I asked him where he was going, and he said he was going to a man's house by the name of Davis. I asked him where Davis lived, and he said he did not know whether it was the first or second house. I asked him where he was going from there, and he said he was going down on some creek to get him a horse. I forget the place. I then arrested him and sent one of the men into headquarters with him."

An officer that had stepped up next to the sergeant snapped to attention and said, "My name is 1ˢᵗ Lieutenant Stopral with the 1ˢᵗ Missouri Cavalry. On the evening of the 29th of last month, I was in my office. The prisoner was brought before me by one of our pickets. I asked the prisoner if he had any pass, and he said not. I asked him if he had any papers whatsoever to be identified, and he said not. I told him he certainly must have something with him either books or papers, and he then produced a memoranda book. The one here marked 'A' is the one he showed me. Inside I found the following telegraphic writing that I easily translated as the following, '3rd Ohio Battery has 4 guns - brass, 11th Ohio Battery has 6 guns - brass. Three brigades of cavalry in a division. Three regiments in a brigade, brigade commanded by Davidson. Infantry: 1st Brigade has 3 regiments. 2nd Brigade has 3 regiments, one on detached service - 1 battery 4 pieces Parrott guns. Brig. General Soloman commands a division, two brigades in a division; three regiments in one brigade, two in the other. Two batteries in the division. 'I gave the book to Captain George Hanna and sent the prisoner to the guard house."

David O. Dodd

Stonewall Jackson

(Hospital)

"Read that again," Peg insisted.

"On January 8, 1864, a bitterly cold day when the Arkansas River was frozen solid, Dodd was hanged on the grounds of his former school, St. John's, just east of the Little Rock Arsenal before horrified onlookers who had crossed the river to witness his execution. The hangman's rope stretched, and the boy dangled, strangling to death over a full five minutes. Onlookers as well as Union soldiers became ill at the tragic spectacle." Patch paused for a long moment then continued, "David O. Dodd is buried in the southeast portion of Mount Holly Cemetery in Little Rock. An eight-foot marble monument at the boy's grave is engraved, 'Here lie the remains of David O. Dodd. Born in Lavaca County, Texas, Nov. 10, 1846, died Jan. 8, 1864. 'Nearby is a marble scroll with the words, 'Boy Martyr of the Confederacy.'"

Peg looked away and sniffed. "He's my hero." Peg sniffed again. "David O. Dodd, David O. Dodd, David O. Dodd. I want to remember that poor boy's name." Peg sniffed again. "David Owen Dodd."

PHILAD
N.Y. AND
BALTIMORE
PAPERS

CHAPTER 11 - THE RED RIVER CAMPAIGN

(Hospital)

Abby smiled at Patch and said, "I promised you I would bring in a Poe book." She picked up the book in her lap and read aloud, "Edgar Allan Poe was born January 19, 1809, in Boston, Massachusetts. He died October 7, 1849, in Baltimore, Maryland. He was an accomplished American short-story writer, poet, critic, and editor who was famous for his cultivation of mystery and the macabre. He focused on literary genres different from those of his contemporaries - the short story and short poem. His work reflected his own pessimistic outlook on life and focused chiefly on the mental state of the characters. He is credited with pioneering detective fiction in such stories as the 'Murders in the Rue Morgue, '1843 and gothic horror in the 'Fall of the House of Usher, '1839 and the 'Tell-Tale Heart, '1843. His 'The Raven, '1845, numbers among the best-known poems in the national literature."

"Can you read some of 'The Raven 'and let me compare it with Emerson's 'The Humble Bee?'" Patch asked, putting down his newspaper.

"Yep." Abby cleared her throat and read, "'The Raven 'by Edgar Allan Poe."

'Once upon a midnight dreary, while I pondered, weak and weary,
Over many a quaint and curious volume of forgotten lore —
While I nodded, nearly napping, suddenly there came a tapping, As of someone gently rapping, rapping at my chamber

door.
"'Tis some visitor," I muttered, "tapping at my chamber door —
        Only this and nothing more."

'Ah, distinctly I remember it was in the bleak December;
And each separate dying ember wrought its ghost upon the floor.
Eagerly I wished the morrow; — vainly I had sought to borrow
From my books surcease of sorrow — sorrow for the lost Lenore
—

For the rare and radiant maiden whom the angels name Lenore
—

        Nameless here for evermore.

'And the silken, sad, uncertain rustling of each purple curtain
Thrilled me — filled me with fantastic terrors never felt before;
So that now, to still the beating of my heart, I stood repeating
"'Tis some visitor entreating entrance at my chamber door —
Some late visitor entreating entrance at my chamber door; —
        This it is and nothing more."

'Presently my soul grew stronger; hesitating then no longer,
"Sir," said I, "or Madam, truly your forgiveness I implore;
But the fact is I was napping, and so gently you came rapping,
And so faintly you came tapping, tapping at my chamber door,
That I scarce was sure I heard you" — here I opened wide the
door; ——
        Darkness there and nothing more.

'Deep into that darkness peering, long I stood there wondering,
fearing,
Doubting, dreaming dreams no mortal ever dared to dream
before;
But the silence was unbroken, and the stillness gave no token,
And the only word there spoken was the whispered word,
"Lenore?"
This I whispered, and an echo murmured back the word,
"Lenore!" —

Merely this and nothing more.

'Back into the chamber turning, all my soul within me burning,
Soon again I heard a tapping somewhat louder than before.
"Surely," said I, "surely that is something at my window lattice;
Let me see, then, what thereat is, and this mystery explore —
Let my heart be still a moment and this mystery explore;—
  'Tis the wind and nothing more!"

'Open here I flung the shutter, when, with many a flirt and
flutter,
In there stepped a stately Raven of the saintly days of yore;
Not the least obeisance made he; not a minute stopped or stayed
he;
But, with mien of lord or lady, perched above my chamber door
—
Perched upon a bust of Pallas just above my chamber door —
  Perched, and sat, and nothing more.

'Then this ebony bird beguiling my sad fancy into smiling,
By the grave and stern decorum of the countenance it wore,
"Though thy crest be shorn and shaven, thou," I said, "art sure no
craven,
Ghastly grim and ancient Raven wandering from the Nightly
shore —
Tell me what thy lordly name is on the Night's Plutonian shore!"
  Quoth the Raven "Nevermore."'

Just then, a black orderly leaned his head around the tent door
and cleared his throat, "Miss Abby, your momma is wait'n for
you's in her carriage."

Abby jumped up and patted Hunter on his sleeping forehead. "O'
my goodness! There is still so much more to this beautiful poem
by Edgar Allan Poe, but I must go," Abby said, picking up her
other unread books

"Edgar Allan Poe?" Peg said, twisting his face and looking

quizzically at Patch.

"If you don't know who he is, shame on you. If I don't tell you who he is, shame on me," Abby said over her shoulder as she disappeared out the tent door, "I'll see you boys later."

"Well, put that in your pipe, and smoke it my skinny, bearded, ruminant friend." Patch laughed and smiled to himself.

Peg looked at the empty doorway for a long moment. Finally, he slowly turned to Patch, fluttered his eyelashes, smiled a toothy grin and said, "So, tell me what thy lordly name is - Mr. Patch or should I quote the raven 'Nevermore?'"

"How about 'never mind?'" Patch ignored Peg as he thumbed absently through the newspaper and then stopped, folded the newspaper back and commented, "This is interesting. Here is a long article about the Red River Campaign."

"What's that?" Peg asked, still fluttering his eyelashes and smiling his toothy grin.

"It says here that the Yankees 'Red River Campaign had three goals. One was to destroy the Confederate Army commanded by Kirby-Smith and Taylor. The second was to capture Shreveport, Louisiana, and crush the war-making machine called the Trans-Mississippi Department of the Confederacy. And the third was to capture the cotton for the idle mills in Massachusetts, where 28,000 mill workers were out of a job."

"What does General Lincoln care about cotton mills?" Peg mumbled around a dirty finger he had stuck into his mouth to dislodge tobacco stuck between his cheek and gums. "He has a war to fight."

"He also had a new election to win, and voters to woo. So, he wanted the thousands of bales of cotton from the plantations along the Red River."

"Humph," Peg snorted and spit into the brass spittoon.

"Mr. Lincoln and his Generals knew that Texas was the source of much needed guns, food, and supplies for Confederate troops. They knew that the occupation of east Texas and especially the control of the Red River would separate and isolate Texas from the rest of the Confederacy." Patch read to himself for a moment and continued, "Get this. There was also some concern that the 25,000 French troops in Mexico sent by Napoleon III and under the command of Emperor Maximillian might join forces with Confederate troops in Texas and use the Red River Valley as a point of entry to reinforce Confederate troops in the Trans-Mississippi Department and then move east, across the Mississippi River."

"Indian soldiers, blacks soldiers and now 25,000 French soldiers?" Peg started to puff up.

"I know. I know," Patch interrupted. "What happened to the gentleman's war?" Without waiting for an answer, Patch continued. "It looks like the Yankee's plan was for General Nathaniel P. Banks sitting in New Orleans to march his 20,000 troops 330 miles up the Red River toward Shreveport while

Admiral Porter and his 23-ship flotilla with thirteen gunboats, six of them ironclad, came down the Mississippi from Vicksburg to the mouth of the Red River and then up the river toward Shreveport, a 350-mile trip. A General Smith and his 15,000 troops were to accompany Admiral Porter from Vicksburg." Patch paused then added, "Interesting. Smith and his 15,000 men were on 30-day loan from General Sherman, who intended to use them to help with his planned march to the sea."

"Sherman, the crazy red head," Peg grumbled.

"Crazy like a fox!" Patch exclaimed, paused for a moment, and then smiled. "Get this. The third prong of the Yankee offensive was General Steele. His orders were to leave Little Rock with 7,000 Yankee troops, march 200 miles down through southwest Arkansas and attack Shreveport from the north."

"March down through southwest Arkansas," Peg repeated. "March down through Benton, Rockport, Malvern, Arkadelphia, Prescott and Camden." He blinked. "March down through Washington, the new capital of the Confederacy in Arkansas?"

"It does seem crazy to march Yankees right through the middle of where the army of Arkansas is camped out, waiting for 'Do Something 'orders from the Trans-Mississippi Department of the Confederacy," Patch added. "But I don't write the news, Peg. I just read it."

"Well, good luck," Peg snorted as he vigorously rubbed his hands together as if warming them over an open campfire. "Those good old boys ain't had nothing to do since Marmaduke chewed up Pine Bluff and came back to Camden with all that Yankee booty." Peg shifted confidently in his chair and predicted, "General Steele and his Yankees will never make it through that Rebel gauntlet let alone make it to Shreveport to crush the Trans-Mississippi war making machine."

"Thank you for that insight General Peg." Patch looked down at the newspaper and read, "Fort DeRussy was the first battle on the Red River, where 350 Confederate soldiers behind an iron-armored gun battery tried to fight off 15,000 Yankees and a 23-ship flotilla, with thirteen gunboats, six of them ironclad."

"Who won?" Peg asked.

Patch avoided the question and continued, "General Banks got a telegram from General Grant reminding him that Smith and his 15,000 Yankees were on loan for only 30 days, so do something." Patch read for a moment and continued, "With that pressure on him, General Banks pushed his soldiers up the river to Grand Ecore, only 75 miles south of Shreveport. Admiral Porter followed, forcing his ships over the treacherous falls at Alexandria. Grand Ecore General Banks made two big mistakes. First, the road to Shreveport veered away from the river and the support from the cannons of the flotilla. Second, Banks didn't scout out what he was heading into further up that road. At Mansfield, 50 miles away from the river, the Rebel fell on the Yankees in great numbers and won the Battle of Mansfield handily. The Yankees were forced to retreat 30 miles down to Pleasant Hill where they successfully warded off the Rebel hordes at the Battle of Pleasant Hill. Even though the Yankees at the end of the day held the field of battle, at nightfall, they slinked away in the dark and marched the 30 miles back to Grand Ecore and the support of the flotilla."

"No-tilla the flo-tilla is ro-tilla," Peg howled and slapped his good knee.

"I don't have the slightest idea what all that means, but if it means the flotilla is in trouble, you are right." Patch adjusted the paper. "On the Red River, Admiral Porter was battling low water, continual Confederate harassment and obstructions at Loggy Bayou. He got within 30 miles of Shreveport, but because of the lack of any further progress, the admiral decided to go back down river and regroup at Grand Ecore. En route the

Confederates surprised Porter's squadron from the riverbank at Blair's Plantation, inflicted little damage on the vessels but showed they had the initiative."

"No-tilla the flo-tilla is ro-tilla," Peg howled again, slapped his good knee and did a little shuffle in his chair.

"It says here that unbeknownst to General Banks, the Confederate commander in charge, General Kirby-Smith, had dispatched three infantry divisions to Arkansas to stop the Yankees headed to Shreveport. This, unfortunately, left General Taylor with a reduced force of only 5,000 men, too few to carry out his desire to capture all of the Yankees, their flotilla and all their powder, guns and supplies. Instead, he was left with only harassing the Union forces as they began to withdraw the 60 miles back down to Alexandria."

Edmund Kirby Smith

Nathaniel P Banks

"No-tilla, General Banks and the flo-tilla are ro-tilla."

"Peg, will you give that a rest?" Patch said, getting slightly annoyed.

"Sorry. I just like the sound of the word 'flotilla'. Flotilla. Flotilla. Flotilla. Flotilla," Peg said, twisting his mouth a dozen different ways. "Flotilla."

"It looks like Admiral Porter is in a pickle. Because of the lack of rain and low water, he could not get his flotilla…" Patch fish-eyed Peg before he could say anything and continued, "He could not get his squadron over the rocks and falls at Alexandria."

(Dream)

The young Lieutenant Colonel standing next to Hunter pushed him angrily into Mr. Bailey, who was standing next to Hunter in the semi-circle of officers. With ever increasing anger, he stomped on the stack of sticks Bailey had carefully constructed in the dirt. "That is the most outlandish suggestion I have ever heard." He turned smartly to Admiral Porter. "Sir, if you listen to this lunatic, he will get us all killed, captured or both."

Admiral Porter stood silent for a long moment and then looked up at the young Lieutenant Colonel. "That was Mr. Bailey's plan, sir. What would you have us do?"

The young Lieutenant Colonel sucked in his stomach and puffed out his chest in a defiant gesture toward Lieutenant Colonel Bailey. "Sir, I would scuttle the flotilla, put it to the torch and march out of here with General Banks 'infantry."

"That thought alone pains me greatly, sir," the Admiral said, thoughtfully rubbing his cheek. "I was forced to scuttle the Eastport at Grand Ecore because of torpedo damage. That fact alone saddens me greatly." He mused for a moment then added, "The thought of losing my whole flotilla pains me to the bone."

"Sir, we will all be pained to the bone if we are all rotting somewhere

in a Confederate prison." He cleared his nervous-voice and added, "We have all heard reports of the deplorable conditions at the Andersonville prison camp in southwest Georgia."

The Admiral held up his hand for silence and turned toward Lieutenant Colonel Bailey, who quickly jumped to attention. "Sir, I know we can do it, and it will work. I grew up in the woods of Wisconsin. My father and I are lumbermen and have fell trees and stacked them in just this way to dam off creeks and bayous to flood fields or divert rivers so we could repair old bridges or lay footings for new ones." He paused then added confidently, "Trust me. I know it will work."

The young Lieutenant Colonel standing next to Hunter stomped what sticks were left from Bailey's construction and ground them angrily into the dust. Now, almost screaming with agitation, the young officer turned to the admiral. "Sir, this is not some muddy creek-bottom or lazy bayou. This is a wide, wild rushing torrent of water, treacherous to navigate and impossible to contain. I say let's abandon this lunatic's scheme and get out of here before they collect more Rebel troops from Texas and capture all of us."

The admiral turned to General Banks. "Sir, what do you think?"

"It will either work, or I will drag you out of here when we leave." General Banks playfully patted the admiral on the back. "Hunter, light the Admiral's cigar."

(Hospital)

"Read that again," Peg insisted.

"It says thanks must go to the bright and resourceful chief engineer from the 19th Corps, who came up with a plan to save the day. Lieutenant Colonel Joseph Bailey, the 19th Corps's chief engineer, organized Banks 'men into work teams. For ten days, 10,000 troops worked feverishly on both banks of the river to build the dam. Slowly, the river began to rise. But success was not to be had so easily." Patch paused to sip his coffee and looked at Peg, who was leaning so far out of his chair, a sneeze or cough would put him on the hospital tent's dirt floor. Patch read quickly, "Upon seeing a 66 foot gash in the middle of the dam rip open, Admiral Porter leaped on a horse and galloped upstream. He ordered four boats to shoot the chute before the water level began to fall. Three of the boats were moored at the banks and had to start their engines. The oldest boat of the fleet, the Lexington, put on a full head of steam, passed over the remaining rocks of the channel, and headed for the 66-foot opening. On the banks, 30,000 soldiers and sailors watched."

"The admiral wrote later in his report, 'The Lexington steered directly for the opening in the dam, through which the water was rushing so furiously that it seemed as if nothing but destruction awaited her. Thousands of beating hearts looked on, anxious for the result. The silence was so great as the Lexington approached the dam that a pin might almost be heard to fall. She entered the gap with a full head of steam on, pitched down the roaring torrent, made two or three spasmodic rolls, hung for a moment on the rocks below, was then swept into the deep water by the current, and rounded safely into the bank. Thirty thousand voices rose in one deafening cheer, and universal joy seemed to pervade the face of every man present.'"

"Just great!" Peg declared.

"But success was still not to be had so easily. Everyone watched as the rushing nine-mile-an-hour current continued to suck away pieces from the center of the dam. As the water level fell again, Bailey came up with another crafty solution. He and his dam builders went quickly up above the rapids and in three days built a tidal-block across part of the river to slow the rushing current down. Once they did that and closed the growing gash in the center of the dam, the river once again started rising above the stony rapids."

"Where are our sharpshooters all this time?" Peg complained. "Sitting around picking their teeth and swatting mosquitoes?"

"Busy," Patch offered reassuringly. "But every time one Yankee sharpshooters saw a puff of smoke come from the woods, ten Yankee sharpshooters from the boats would return fire."

"Ten? Great!"

"Finally, the river rose high enough for all the ships to get over and pass the treacherous rapids. Once past the rocks of the rapids, Bailey dynamited the dam and the flotilla continued on down river effortlessly." Patched sipped his coffee and continued, "Cleverness, however, didn't end there for the young lieutenant. When the Union infantry marched down to the Atchafalaya River, they discovered that the river was blocking their retreat. Bailey's ingenuity again came to the rescue. He cleverly constructed a floating bridge by aligning the naval vessels side-by-side and connecting them with heavy planks."

"Great. What were the Rebels doing during this retreat?" Peg railed.

"It says here that Taylor's greatly reduced Confederate forces continued harassing the retreating Federal troops the best they could, unsuccessfully engaging them at Mansura, Louisiana, and at Yellow Bayou."

"That 'greatly reduced Confederate forces 'is all thanks to Kirby-Smith's sending three infantry divisions to Arkansas. He's got the 'divide and conquer' thing twisted around. You are supposed to divide and conquer your enemy, not your own troops. If you divide your own troops, you conquer nothing." Peg rubbed his beard furiously and added, "I can tell you one thing, if old Marmaduke were there, he would have run old Banks down to the muddy old banks of the mighty Missisip."

"A place where General Banks and his military career should

have avoided," Patch quipped. "Listen to this. General Banks '72-day debacle had cost the Yankees dearly 8,700 killed. It says that General Grant was really, really mad and had General Banks replaced on the spot when he arrived at the 'muddy old banks of the mighty Missisip'. General Edward Canby immediately became the new field commander of the Army of the Gulf. It's reported that Grant felt that, because of the Red River Campaign and the absence of those troops from the eastern theater, his ability to applying stronger pressure on more valuable Confederate targets had been greatly compromised."

Peg scrunched up his face and mewed like a sick cat. "Mew. Mew. Mew. Mew. Mew."

"It says here that the Confederate's lost 6,500 men in the Red River Campaign, and their victories were marginal. Yes, they repelled the Union invasion of Shreveport, but they failed to destroy its columns in Arkansas and in Louisiana." Patch sipped his coffee and added, "It says that General Taylor remained angry and hostile toward General Kirby-Smith over his decision to dispatch three infantry divisions to Arkansas, which all but de-fanged Taylor's ability to crush the Yankees when he had the chance at the treacherous falls at Alexandria." Patch looked at Peg and looked back at his newspaper. "Here's a sad note. It says that Bailey was killed by Bushwhackers at Nevada, Missouri, 75 miles northwest of Springfield and is buried in the Evergreen Cemetery in Fort Scott, Kansas."

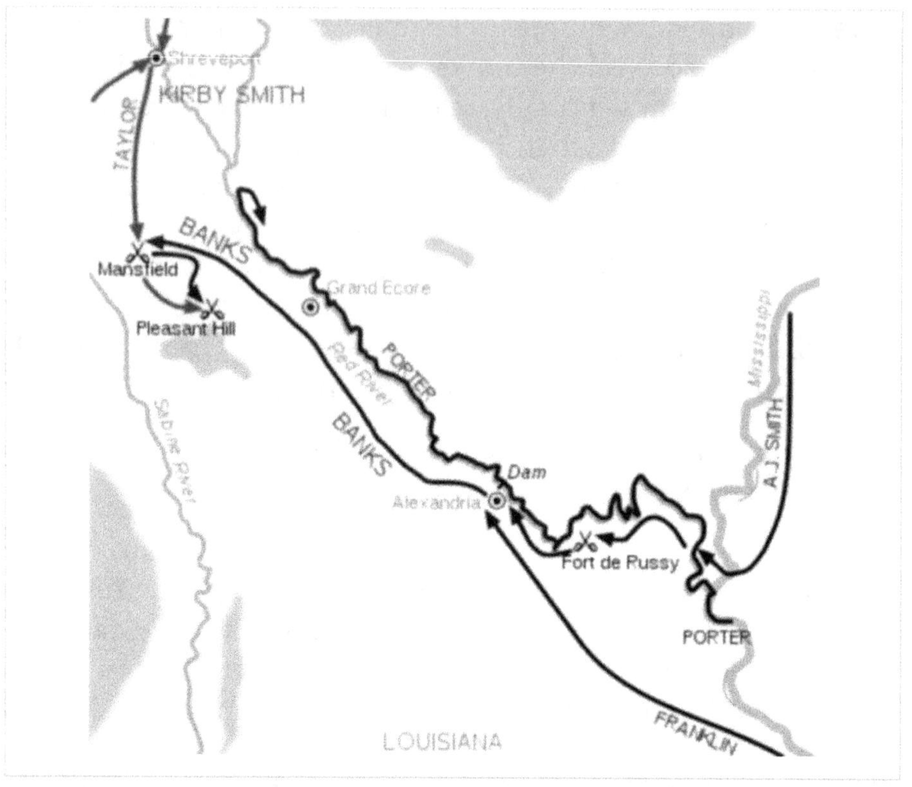

Peg spit a stream of brown juice into the brass spittoon, scrunched up his face and fish-eyed Patch sideways. "What did you call it, 'General Banks '72-day belt-buckle?'"

"Debacle, Peg, not belt-buckle, debacle," Patch corrected his old friend. "It was a 72-day De-Bock-Kull. Debacle means a total failure, often a laughable failure. And the Red River Campaign would have been a laughable failure if the whole thing wasn't so sad and so many lives lost."

Peg turned to the sleeping Hunter and said, "Hunter, hand me de-buckle to put on de-belt to wear with de-shirt and de-pants." Peg laughed at his own joke as he slapped his good knee.

Patched sipped his coffee while he waited for Peg to calm down.

Peg finally sniffed a long sniff and wiped a tear from his eye. "De-buckle, de-bock-kull, debacle, de-buckle." Peg snickered a little again and then cleared his throat. "Sometimes I hurt myself." With that, he slapped his good knee and started laughing all over again.

CHAPTER 12 - THE CAMDEN EXPEDITION

(Hospital)

Abby picked up one of the books in her lap, opened to the back of it and read aloud, "Oliver Wendell Holmes Senior was born August 29, 1809, and became a successful doctor, speaker and author. In 1841, his wife berthed Holmes Junior, who served with honor in the Civil War. He was gravely wounded in battle three separate times, once taking a bullet through the neck at the battle of Antietam. He later studied law and became a very successful attorney." Abby looked at Patch and added, "A famous man who had an equally famous son."

"In 1858, Holmes Senior helped found the magazine Atlantic Monthly, and for many years, he wrote the magazine's popular feature 'The Autocrat of the Breakfast Table,' whose protagonist held forth at an imaginary Boston boarding house, dishing up witty opinions on an endless variety of subjects."

"In 1830, Oliver Wendell Holmes 'patriotic poem 'Old Ironsides' helped prevent the scrapping of the historic battleship U.S.S. Constitution, launched in 1797 and condemned in 1828. In the War of 1812, it vanquished the British frigate Guerrière. Tradition holds that it was nicknamed by sailors who saw the British cannonballs failing to penetrate its oak sides." Abby cleared her throat and read aloud, "'Old Ironsides 'by Oliver Wendell Holmes, Senior.

"'Ay, tear her tattered ensign down! / Long has it waved on high, / And many an eye has danced to see / That banner in the sky; / Beneath it rung the battle shout, / And burst the cannon's roar; / The meteor of the ocean air / Shall sweep the clouds no more!'"

'"Her deck, once red with heroes' blood, / Where knelt the vanquished foe, / When winds were hurrying o'er the flood / And waves were white below, / No more shall feel the victor's tread, / Or know the conquered knee; / The harpies of the shore shall pluck / The eagle of the sea!'"

'"Oh, better that her shattered hulk / Should sink beneath the wave; / Her thunders shook the mighty deep, / And there should be her grave; / Nail to the mast her holy flag, / Set every threadbare sail, / And give her to the God of storms, / The lightning and the gale!'"

Just then a black orderly leaned his head around the tent door and cleared his throat, "Miss Abby, your momma is wait'n for you's in her carriage."

Abby jumped up and patted Hunter on his sleeping forehead. "I'll see you boys later," she said over her shoulder as she disappeared out the tent door.

"Wow! What a powerful and moving poem." Peg spit a stream of brown juice into the brass spittoon and wiped his mouth with the sleeve of his shirt. "That is good stuff from Old Wendell, even if his son did fight for the Yankees."

"Peg, there are good people on both sides of this thing," Patch offered while thumbing through the new newspaper Abby had delivered to him. "This is interesting," he said, folding the newspaper back. "Here is a long article about General Steele's Camden Expedition."

"What's that?"

"I don't know," Patch said honestly. "Maybe this will tell us." Patch read quietly to himself for a moment then added, "It says here preparatory to starting his march from Little Rock to

Shreveport to help General Banks win his Red River Campaign, General Steele had his Colonel Clayton move 1,100 Yankees from Pine Bluff to cut off Rebel troops rumored to have departed from Monticello." Patch read quietly then added, "The paper is calling it the action at Mount Elba. It is credited with creating the desired disruption to allow General Steele to advance south from Little Rock unmolested. Geez, 417 Rebels soldiers were captured or killed during the engagement at Mount Elba."

"Man, 417 Rebels soldiers captured or killed. That's not good news." Peg rubbed his beard thoughtfully.

"But it wasn't all good news for the Yankees either. It says that Steele's headaches with his Camden Expedition started when he left Little Rock with 8,500 men and wagons. Muddy roads slowed his march down to Benton and Rockport. He crossed the Ouachita River and marched down to Arkadelphia. There he waited three days for General Thayer and his 3,600 troops from Fort Smith. However, they were a no-show, so Steele started to march southwest without them toward Washington, the new state capital."

Gen. Sterling Price Old Pap

Gen. Frederick Steele

"What is Granny Holmes doing all this time?" Peg asked quizzically.

"Remember, General Holmes fell ill after Helena and was replaced by General Price, Pap Price? Well, Price has been busy. When the 8,500 Yankees left Little Rock, they became a moving target for the Confederate Army of Arkansas. General Pap sent Colonel Greene to badger the column's left flank. Colonel Shelby was sent around to nip at the column's heels, and Marmaduke's cavalry was sent to punch at the head of the moving column with hit and fall-back tactics."

"Wow, it sounds like they stumbled into a Rebel beehive," Peg hooted and howled as he continued a little jig in his chair. "Red River Campaign or no Red River Campaign, it is a bad idea to march Yankee troops across the southwest corner of Arkansas. That's where all the Rebels are bunched up. They have been driven out of every other corner of the state. Now they are just standing behind the door waiting for the Yankees to march through, so they can jump out and holler 'SURPRISE.'" Peg paused and then added, "A beehive. They have stumbled into a Rebel beehive." He hooted and howled again as he continued a little jig in his chair.

Patch read quietly to himself for a moment and then added, "Steele had left a brigade of infantry at Okolona, about five miles from Elkin's Ferry, to protect his rear and to watch and wait for Thayer's 3,600 troops. However, our Colonel Shelby spotted this isolated Yankee unit and jumped them."

(Dream)

Colonel Shelby's spirited horse was nervous and rattled by the waves of stinging fist-sized hail now noisily beating up the pine trees that they had run to once the freezing rain turned to balls of ice. Hunter had a difficult time keeping the horse from bolting out from under the overhanging limbs of protection. "Hold her steady, boy." Colonel Shelby ordered, as he stood tall in his stirrups to watch the battle.

Hunter shivered, and his teeth chattered amid the jar of the thunder, the flash of the lighting and the moaning and singing of the pines as the hailstorm tore noisily through them. All this was mingled with the crash of artillery, the sharp rattle of musketry, the wild blare of bugles and the ringing clash of sabers. Colonel Shelby slid effortlessly from his horse and stood next to Hunter. He took a deep breath of the cold air, moved his hand in a wide sweeping arch, and turned to Hunter smiling, "This is rugged and sublime."

Suddenly, the cannons and muskets fell silent. Hunter turned to Colonel Shelby with a blank look on his face. Just as he did, dozens of Rebel soldiers came tearing through the pine forest. Shelby grabbed one of the men who was flailing at himself and hollered into his face, "What's wrong with you, soldier?"

"Sir, we can stand the hissing and whining of Yankee bullets, but we can't stand the stinging of thousands of bees."

(Hospital)

"Read that again," Peg insisted.

"It says the Battle of Okolona, also known as the Elkin's Ferry Engagement, raged on for over three hour until suddenly a thunderstorm moved into the area. It lit up the skies with blinding flashes of lightning, punctuated with teeth rattling peals of thunder, all mixed with the belching of cannons and the sharp rattle of musketry. Just as suddenly, the thunderstorm turned into a hailstorm. It is not for sure if it was the musket fire, the cannon fire or the hailstorm, but something dislodged a number of beehives causing thousands of bees to sweep over the field of battle - silencing the guns and scattering the soldiers in all directions."

"I told you it was a bad idea to march Yankees across the southwest corner of the state. They did and what happened? They stumbled into a Rebel beehive," Peg hollered and did a little jig in his chair. "Skedaddle from the battle," Peg snorted and added, "The Battle of the Bees."

Patch took a sip of his coffee and waited for Peg to quiet down before continuing. "While Steele's men were fighting a rearguard action, he was trying to get the rest of his troops across the Little Missouri River just down from Elkin's Ferry. Just about the time half of them got across, Marmaduke's cavalry fell on them. The fighting favored the South until the rest of the Yankee column crossed the river and joined the tired and beleaguered troops trying to fight off Marmaduke's advances. After that, the tide turned to the Federals 'favor."

"My main man Marmaduke is munching on the marchers," Peg snickered and sniffed while he vigorously rubbed his hands together as if warming them over an open campfire.

"Marmaduke fell back to Prairie D'Ane to rest and regroup. General Price and the rest of his Camden garrison, two brigades of cavalry headed up by General Dockery and Colonel Crawford, joined him. Later that day, these troops were joined by 1,500 men composed of Texans and Choctaw Indians led by Colonel Gano."

Patch, avoiding Peg's sideways stare, calmly took a sip of his coffee and added, "General Thayer with his 3,600 rag-tag bunch of Yankees from Fort Smith finally showed up, tired and hungry. These 3,600 hungry mouths put an even further strain on Steele's meager supplies. His own troops had been living on half rations for days. He sent an urgent message back to Little Rock to send food."

"Hey, we lived on half rations during the Mexican American War, and pretty soon all you can think about is food," Peg offered.

"It got worse for the Yankees. Remember it had been hailing and storming. Well, the Yankee's march was now marred by deep mud and swollen streams. So after the mauling they suffered at Elkins 'Ferry, Steele decided to give up on the idea of joining up with General Banks and his Red River Campaign. Instead, he decided to turn south and march on Camden, 50 miles away, and look for food."

"And our General Price?"

"He mistakenly assumed that the Yankees would go straight and march the 25 miles to attack Washington. So he moved his men and positioned them at Prairie D'Ane, about half way between Elkins 'Ferry and the new capital. General Steele was clever. He knew Camden was heavily fortified, so he moved some of his men toward Prairie D'Ane and skirmished with the Rebels there, as if his goal really was to capture the capital. The politicians in Washington were frantic and insistent upon more protection, so Price all but emptied Camden of troops. While the Confederates prepared for the attack on the capital, Steele and his troops turned south to march toward Camden instead." Patch sipped his coffee and continued, "Realizing that the Yankee's desire was Camden and not the new capital, Price sent his cavalry and the Second Indian Brigade to attack the departing Yankees. However, at the little village of Moscow, on the edge of Prairie

D'Ane, the Yankees had set up their artillery to fend off the attack. Once in place and booming loudly, the artillery decisively halted the attack. One Union officer explained: 'It is well known that the savages are much afraid of 'big guns, 'and a few shots from our artillery soon sent them to the right about.'" Patch looked sideways at Peg and continued quickly, "Once the attack was squelched, the Yankees walked into Camden unmolested, unmolested but hungry. Their bellies were talking to their backbones."

"Man, I know that feeling," Peg declared and moaned a little.

"The supplies that were ordered a week earlier never showed up. But Steele found out from local Union sympathizers where the Confederates had stanched away 5,000 bushels of corn. He immediately sent out a foraging party of 200 wagons and 1,200 men. However, Confederate lookouts spotted the approaching Union wagon train and managed to burn about 1,500 bushels before being run off."

"And Price is going to let them just have what corn was left?" Peg looked blankly at Patch.

"I don't think so. It says that Price had his men watching every road in and out of Camden specifically watching for foraging parties." Patch paused, took a sip of coffee and continued, "Marmaduke, with 12 cannons and 3,600 men, 700 of whom were Choctaw and Chickasaw Indians, slipped into position at a place called Poison Spring, about 14 miles away from Camden and waited."

"My man Marmaduke is about to spring into action at Poison Spring," Peg declared loudly. "And the Yankees didn't even see it coming."

"When the Rebels jumped them, the Yankee commander Colonel Williams quickly grouped his wagons and men. He had 400 black infantrymen from the First Kansas Colored Volunteers, mostly former slaves from Missouri and Arkansas. He put them in the center of his formation and positioned his cavalry on his right and left flank. Marmaduke came right up the middle and hit the black infantrymen hard and fast. They fought courageously, but within three hours, half of them were dead. The Yankee cavalry on the right and left flanks were eventually overrun. As the Rebels pressed the attack, the Yankees scattered and fled to a marsh and the safety of its thick trees."

(Dream)

General Maxey pushed Hunter out of the way and got right into General Marmaduke's face. "I outrank you, sir, and I order you to stand down."

Marmaduke took a slight step back from the angry general. "I have fresh cavalry units here which have seen only limited action. I implore you to let us continue our sweep, and we will crush the fleeing Bluecoats."

General Maxey grabbed the reins out of Hunter's hands and handed them to Marmaduke. "I order you to stand down."

Marmaduke threw the reins back at Hunter. "We have 200 captured wagons loaded with forage and four Yankee field pieces. It would only take a handful of my men to escort the wagons back to Price's headquarters near Woodlawn. So I implore you to let us press the attack and drive the Yankees out of the woods."

General Maxey again grabbed the reins out of Hunter's hands. "Sir, those supplies are more important than a handful of Yankees." He handed the reins to Marmaduke. "I want those wagons and supplies protected in case General Steele decides to send hoards of Yankees from Camden to reclaim his losses."

Marmaduke threw the reins back at Hunter. "But, sir. We have one full regiment from Cabell's brigade watching the road from Camden to prevent any Federal surprise." Marmaduke raised his hands, palms up, as if in disbelief and added angrily, "Again, I implore you to allow a full scale pursuit of the fleeing Federals."

General Maxey grabbed the reins out of Hunter's hand and handed them to Marmaduke. "I order you to get out of here."

(Hospital)

Peg rubbed his beard furiously and sniped. "Wow, 200 wagons. What did General Steele think about those potatoes?"

"He was not too happy. Even though Williams and his men escaped, they still lost 1,200 mules and four cannons. Plus, Williams lost 30 percent of his white troops and 42 percent of his black troops." Patch sucked his teeth for a second then continued, "It was reported that even though the Choctaw and Chickasaw Indians went on a scalping party, many of the former slaves, who lay wounded on the field of battle, were massacred by non-Indians."

Peg spit a stream of brown juice into the brass spittoon and wiped his mouth with the sleeve of his shirt. "Jeez, 1,200 mules, that's bad news. You can build a wagon in a couple of hours but you need a couple of years to replace a working mule."

"Well, Steele got more bad news," Patch said and then added, "The supply wagon train from Pine Bluff finally arrived but with only ten days of supplies on board. The real bad news, however, was that General Banks and his Yankee troops got chewed up in Louisiana at the Battle of Mansfield and the Battle of Pleasant Hill. And the Confederates had the Yankees on the run back to Alexandra where their fleet was hung up on the rocks, high and dry."

"Well, so much for the Red River Campaign," Peg railed. "Has Steele given up on his Camden Expedition?"

"Not yet. He sent Lt. Colonel Drake with 240 empty wagons guarded by 1,400 troops back to Pine Bluff for more food." Patch sipped his coffee and then added, "Our General Fagan learned of the wagon train leaving Camden and waited until it got 40 miles out of town. At Marks 'Mills, his 4,000 men, led by Shelby and Cabell, jumped the Federals. Cabell hit them head-on, and Shelby surprised them by coming up boldly on their left flank. The battle ranged on for five hours. Drake received a nasty thigh wound and finally surrendered his Yankee troops, wagons, horses and mules. Even though the 240 wagons were empty, the Rebels profited by stripping the dead soldiers of the clothes and boots and the live soldiers of everything they had in their pocket including their guns and ammunition."

"War's hell," Peg lamented. "What did General Steele think about those potatoes?"

"Steele got news that the three infantry divisions dispatched to Arkansas by General Kirby-Smith, to stop the Yankees headed to Shreveport, were now nearing Camden. So, in the middle of the night, General Steele and his troops wisely snuck out of town and headed back to Little Rock. But, like their trip from Little Rock, their trip back to Little Rock was harassed with the same Rebel persistence. Their heels were continuously nipped at, as their flank was bruised and battered. Like an angry bull being harassed by hungry coyotes, Steele stopped a dozen times to turn and run off his pursuers. He stopped and nipped back savagely at Princeton, at the Ouachita River crossing, at the Saline Bottoms and at Whitmore's Mill. But his progress was again impeded by heavy rains and never-ending mud."

"It sounds like we've got him on the run," Peg declared.

"Yep. At Jenkins 'Ferry, about halfway between Camden and Little Rock, the Yankee wagons got bogged down to the axles, and they had to turn and fight." Patch sipped his coffee and continued, "General Churchill sent the Rebel cavalry, under Colonel Greene, in first, quickly followed up by Tappan's infantry. Churchill reported, 'The rain came in torrent and the ground was a sea of knee-deep mud. The Yankees were dug in and fighting from behind log-breastworks. The battle turned in our favor when two brigades of fresh Missouri infantry under General Parsons showed up swelling our numbers to over 4,000 men. Unfortunately, a cane swamp protected the Federal's right flank. Its left flank was protected by a high hill thickly covered in trees. All we could do was come up the middle – and we did, screaming our bone-rattling Rebel yell.'"

Peg slapped his good knee and yelped, "I bet that put the Yankees on the run."

"Yep. But all during the battle the Yankees were busily moving their wagons across the Saline River. When they finally got the last wagon across, the infantry quickly followed and Steele set the platoon bridges on fire so the Rebel could not follow them." Patch paused then added, "And it worked. The Rebels turned around and marched victoriously back to Camden having rid the southwest corner of Arkansas of Yankees."

Peg jumped up and did a little jig, spinning around on his wooden leg and waving his arms around in the air as if he were some giant bird. "We won. We won. We won." He repeated, falling back into his chair winded and red faced.

"You better take it easy Big Bird before you pass out," Patch said, patting his friend's good knee caringly. "Listen to this. Eyewitness reports say when General Steele and his men got back to Little Rock, the General was splashed and splattered with mud from head to foot. And his troops all looked like they had been rolled in mud."

"That's good old Arkansas gumbo-mud. They can take that back to Yankee-ville as a remembrance of how it feels to lose," Peg hooted and did a little jig in his chair as he went looking for his brass spittoon.

"General Bank's Red River Campaign might have fizzled out, and

Steele's Camden Expedition may have blown back in his face. But I don't think we won, and I don't think the Yankees are leaving Little Rock any time soon to go back to Yankee-ville," Patch said to his jubilant friend who wasn't listening or paying any attention.

CHAPTER 13 - DU VALL'S BLUFF, JACKSONPORT & DITCH BAYOU

(Hospital)

Abby sat with a stack of books in her lap. "What do you want to read from today, Mr. Hunter? How about *Moby-Dick* by Herman Melville? He's an interesting author. It says here he was born August 1, 1819, in New York City, and at the age of 22, he sailed on a whaling ship bound for the South Seas. The next year he jumped ship in the Marquesas Islands. And his adventures on the Polynesia islands were the basis of his first novels, *Typee* and *Omoo*. It says *Moby-Dick* is his masterpiece. It is both an intense whaling narrative and a symbolic examination of the problems and possibilities of American democracy." Abby fanned the pages of the thick and added, "Wow, it's pretty long." She laughed and patted him on his shoulder. "You'll be long out of your coma before we could ever get to the end of this book. Let's find something else."

Patch took the book from Abby and offered, "I read somewhere that Herman Melville went on scouting rides with Yankee soldiers in order to get a glimpse of the Civil War soldier's lifestyle before writing his book *Battle Pieces and Aspects of War*."

"I don't have that one, and *Moby-Dick* is just too long to read. Hunter will be back with us before that. I hope and pray."

"Don't we all? Don't we all?" Patch put the book back into her lap.

Abby looked through the stack of books in her lap and held one up. "How about Emily Dickinson?" She opened to the back of the book and read aloud, "Emily Elizabeth Dickinson was born December 10, 1830, in Amherst, Massachusetts. She lives a mostly introverted and reclusive life rarely leaving her room and refusing to greet family guests. Her neighbors called her the lady in white and a little eccentric. The world calls her a great American poet." Abby closed the book and opened it to the first page. "Let's read a poem and see why." She cleared her throat and read the poem's title, "These Are the Days When Birds Come Back." She took a deep breath and read aloud, "These are the days when Birds come back- / A very few-a Bird or two- / To take a backward look. These are the days when skies resume / The old-old sophistries of June- / A blue and gold mistake. Oh fraud that cannot cheat the Bee- / Almost thy plausibility / Induces my belief. Till ranks of seeds their witness bear- / And softly thro' the altered air / Hurries a timid leaf. Oh Sacrament of summer days, / Oh Last Communion in the Haze- / Permit a child to join. Thy sacred emblems to partake- / They consecrated bread to take / And thine immortal wine!"

Abby paused for a moment to catch her breath and then turned to Hunter, "Hunter, I know it's a little hard to understand, but this is what Miss Dickinson is talking about. This poem is about 'Indian summer.' And you know around here snow can be on the ground, but it's so warm outside you don't even need a coat. Miss Dickinson says all the birds have flown south for the winter, but the nice weather fools a few so they return. 'Sophestries 'means something is plausible, but it is misleading. The 'Sophestries of June 'refer to this deception. And 'a blue and gold mistake 'tells us that, though the blue skies are clear, it is winter because the golden grass is still dead. Mother nature is playing tricks that nearly cause everyone to believe the winter could be over until they see that 'timid leaves 'are still falling. The poem is an overview of nature's unpredictability."

Patch cleared his throat and added, "Miss Dickinson relates the changing of the seasons to the way we rush through life. Those who are old," Patch paused and patted Peg on his good leg then continued, "are now taking a 'backward look 'over our lives and realizing it was a mistake to rush through it so quickly. After all, when we are children, we want to be adults, but once we become adults, we want to become children again. It is too late, the 'Last Communion 'or death is in the distance, 'the Haze, 'and we are powerless to stop it."

"Or even slow it down," Peg grumbled.

Just then, a black orderly leaned his head around the tent door and cleared his throat, "Miss Abby, your momma is wait'n for you's in her carriage."

Abby jumped up and patted Hunter on his sleeping forehead. "I'll see you boys later," she said over her shoulder as she disappeared out the tent door.

"'Oh Last Communion in the Haze,'" Peg moaned and shuttered. "Wow. Why do all the poems have to be so dark and morbid?"

"Not all poems are dark and morbid. Some are happy and full of merriment," Patch said, thumbing through his new newspaper and not looking at Peg. "Life is like that. Sometimes it's happy and gay and sometimes dark and morbid."

"Well fill my cup full of that jollity stuff." Peg said, spitting a stream of brown juice into the brass spittoon and wiped his mouth with the sleeve of his shirt. "And I'll take a pass on the dark and morbid meatloaf." He added, adjusting himself more comfortably in his chair.

Patch, not listening or watching Peg, said absently to himself, "Hum, this is interesting. The Rebels flush with their crushing wins over Bank's failed Red River Campaign, and Steele's failed Camden Expedition started moving out of their little pocket in the southwest corner of Arkansas and began getting busy with the business of war again." Patch sipped his coffee and continued, "At Augusta, on the White River, 25 miles south of Jacksonport, Confederate Brigadier General Dandridge McRae was busily recruiting Rebel troops in the area. To stop these activities, Colonel Andrews and 220 Yankee soldiers arrived at Augusta on the steamboat Dove. Andrews left 60 men to guard the boat and took 160 to go looking for McRae. They found him watering his horse at a stream near Fitzhugh Plantation. Unfortunately for the Yankees, when they found him, they also found 545 Rebels soldiers. And the fight was on. The Yankees fought their way back through the Fitzhugh's Woods and back to their boat in Augusta, losing 27 soldiers while the Confederates lost nearly a 100 men. Even though this news severely hindered General McRae's recruiting abilities in the region, harassing Yankees all over the state escalated." Patch sipped his coffee and continued. "An important Yankee supply line goes by rail from Little Rock east to Du Vall's Bluff on the White River, then down the White River to the Arkansas River, then down to the Mississippi River, then to Memphis. Our man Shelby and his men love to harass and disrupt the flow of supplies along this 100-mile route. And when General Steele emptied out Jacksonport and moved those Yankees down to Du Vall's Bluff to stop the harassment, Shelby moved our boys back into Batesville and Jacksonport, where the Black River joins the White River."

"That sounds good," Peg chuckled.

"Not too good," Patch corrected.

(Dream)

General Shelby grabbed the cigar out of Hunter's mouth, angered at how long the young boy was taking to light it. He popped the cigar into his own mouth, stormed over to the fireplace, found a thin piece of hot kindling, picked it up by the cool end and put the burning end to the tip of his cigar. As he puffed, he looked suspiciously over the tip of his cigar at a nicely dressed sutler.

"Hunter, get this cotton speculator a chair," Shelby said around lengthy puffs at getting his cigar lit.

"General, I'm not a cotton speculator, sir. I deal in fine drink and

tobacco products."

The general took a deep drag on his cigar and coughed a little as he exhaled. "Not too fine of tobacco products, sir." The general offered as he sat down behind his desk and coughed a little more. He cleared his throat and added, "With the taste of these things, maybe you should consider a career as a cotton speculator." He coughed again. "What's your problem?"

"That's my problem, sir." The sutler took the chair Hunter handed him. "With all the thugs and Bushwhackers roaming the countryside, it is hard to make an honest living selling good products."

"Honest?" General Shelby laughed. "The citizens are complaining that butter is five dollars a pound. Coffee is six dollars and eighty cents a pound. Corn is ten dollars a bushel and calico, which sold for a dime before the war, is now selling for five dollars a yard."

"That's the problem. Us sutlers depend on a precarious transportation system that is victimized by roving bands of outlaws and guerrillas. Therefore the citizenry has to pay dearly for what flour, sugar, tobacco, and similar goods that do get delivered."

"Well, all of that is about to end." The general motioned Hunter over. "Read to this fine gentleman the announcement we were just drafting. This, sir, will be nailed to every tree and fencepost at every crossroad throughout the region. I'm giving notice to every Texan,

Missourian and Arkansan roving through northern Arkansas they have 30 days to report to this army." The general looked at Hunter and ordered, "Read."

Hunter cleared his throat and read, "Hear ye, hear ye. Able body persons, you shall fight for the North or the South. I will enlist you in the Confederate army, or I will drive you into the Federal ranks. You shall not remain idle spectators of a dream enacted before your eyes."

(Hospital)

"Partisan Rangers." Peg spit a stream of brown juice into the brass spittoon. "That is just plain dumb. Who came up with that stupid idea?"

"Your buddy General Hindman who replaced Van Dorn."

"He ain't no buddy of mine or any other Arkansan." Peg spit another stream of brown juice into the brass spittoon and wiped his mouth with the sleeve of his shirt. "And Van Dorn, that's the clown who, after marching our soldiers and cannons off to Tennessee, left us nothing to fight the war with." Peg was getting worked up. "Once they crossed the Mississippi River, they disappeared into the Eastern Campaigns, and Arkansas was left high and dry." He rubbed the palms of his hands together furiously and then threw them open, palms up. "Nothing! That's what Van Dorn left us with. Nothing."

"He left us enough 'war machine 'to give the Yankees fits, especially on the Mississippi."

"Oh yeah! Like what?" Peg twisted his nose at Patch and waited.

"It seems that down near the Arkansas and Louisiana border, in the southeastern tip of Arkansas, there is a particularly nasty twisting portion of the Mississippi River called the Greenville Bends. In this portion of the river, ships have to navigate long river-bends separated by narrow necks of land. Steamships moving slowly upriver, with a top speed of thirteen miles per hour, make good targets. Confederate batteries wait until the ships have passed before firing at their stern, where they are most vulnerable. When the vessels being attacked are out of range and continuing up river, the Confederates quickly move their artillery across the narrow necks to attack the same vessels coming around the river bend."

(Dream)

"Hunter! Hunter!" General Greene hit Hunter on the back with the broad side of his sword to get his attention. "Pull the lanyard, and fire the cannon quickly. We have to move it over there to catch the steamer as it comes around the bend."

Hunter froze. He wanted to follow orders, but he didn't want to shoot anybody. "General I've got the measles and have been kicked in the head by a mule," Hunter whined.

"Ah, shut up." The general snorted as he jerked the lanyard himself. The 8-inch, 65-pound ball, in a whirl of smoke and sparks, whooshed out of the end of the cannon in a deafening boom. Everyone watched as the cannon ball, in a sweeping arch, slowly raced toward the tail end of the fleeing Yankee troop transport. The ball whizzed by the big groaning wooden paddle wheel and slapped the river hard, sending a spray of muddy water all over the side of the lumbering steamer, trying desperately to get beyond the range of the angry cannons.

The General spun around and grabbed Hunter by the face. He leaned in only inches from the tip of his nose and sputtered angrily, "In less than two weeks, I have inflicted heavy damage on river traffic. I engaged 21 boats of all descriptions, of which five gunboats and marine-boats were disabled, five transports badly damaged, one sunk, two burned, and two captured. My loss was only five privates slightly wounded. No guns or horses were hit." The wheezing general took a deep breath and all but spitting into Hunter's face, hissed,

"The river is mine, Hunter. Mine!" The general's thumb and index finger dug into Hunter's cheeks, as his red blustery face, now only inches away, turned even redder and more blustery. "But no thanks to you - now get this cannon over to the other bank. Set it up, and when it's time pull the lanyard." Squeezing Hunter's face harder the general screamed, "PULL! And that's an order!"

(Hospital)

"Well, it seems General Canby has had it with what he calls a 'Rebel nuisance at the Greenville Bends 'and has diverted two Yankee divisions en route to join the Army of the Tennessee. He has asked General Smith to pause long enough to 'clean out the Rebels 'in Chicot County."

"Two divisions to run off our boys from Pee-ko County?" Peg grumbled.

"Close. Chicot County and yes. It says twenty-eight steam vessels quietly landed at Sunnyside Plantation. On board were 6,000 men, including a portion of Colonel Currie's Mississippi Marine Brigade, all under the command of General Andrew Jackson Smith." Patch took a sip of coffee and continued, "But our Colonel Greene got word of it and moved his troops down to Red Leaf at the south end of Lake Chicot and took a stand. When he realized how many Yankees there were coming at him, he pulled his 600 troops and six cannons across Ditch Bayou, burned the bridge and set up his cannons. When the advancing Yankees got within range, there was no place in the open ground for them to seek shelter. They were easily chewed up by musket fire and canister shot, consisting of tin cylinders filled with iron balls packed in sawdust which, when fired, turns a cannon into a giant shotgun. The Rebels kept shooting while some of the Yankees headed downstream looking for a place to cross over and get behind Greene's position. It says that along with the Yankees was Old Abe, a bald eagle carried as a mascot by the Eighth Wisconsin."

"Chew'm up, Mr. Mean Greene, and we'll have Old Abe over for supper," Peg laughed and slapped his good knee.

"General Greene was running low on gunpowder, so he pulled back the ten miles to Lake Village in an orderly manner before the Yankees could outflank him." Patch sipped his coffee and added, "It says by the time the Yankees got to Lake Village, the Rebels had scattered and disappeared."

"They can't kill Johnny Reb if you can't find him," Peg snickered.

"Well, Johnny Reb didn't stay hidden for long," Patch said, folding back the newspaper. "After the Ditch Bayou encounter, the Rebels soldiers harassed the Yankees soldiers all over the state. The Action at Wallace's Ferry saw a 1,000 Rebel cavalrymen raid and burn plantations around Helena that were being operated by the Yankees. The Action at Massard Prairie saw 600 Rebels fall on 200 Yankee soldiers camped eight miles out from Fort Smith as an advanced guard providing early warning for the Union troops garrisoned there at the fort. Later, The Action at Fort Smith saw the same Rebels boldly attack the fort itself. The Action at Ashley's Station, near Du Vall's Bluff, saw 2,500 Rebels swoop in wearing Yankee uniforms and swoop back out after destroying ten miles of railroad track, burning

3,000 bales of hay and twenty hay-cutting machines and capturing hundreds of horses and small arms weapons." Patch sipped his coffee and added, "It says these kinds of harassing hit and run raids, for the Rebels, have replaced the massive battles of earlier war years where row upon row of soldiers would face and fire at row upon row of soldiers."

CHAPTER 14 - PRICE'S EXPEDITION & ANARCHY IN ARKANSAS

(Hospital)

Abby picked up a magazine. "Patch, did you know that Louisa May Alcott worked briefly as a Yankee nurse before she got sick and had to return home, where she wrote about her experiences in 'Hospital Sketches' which launched her professional writing career?" She thumbed absently through the magazine. "This is a girl's magazine she edits called 'Merry's Museum.' I think it's a little too girly for Hunter, so let's find something else to read from."

"Hunter and I don't do girly stuff, Miss Abby," Peg snorted.

Abby smiled and put the magazine down. "Patch, did you know that thanks to Miss Alcott's father they could count as family friends people such as Henry David Thoreau and Ralph Waldo Emerson?"

"How do you know so much about Louisa May Alcott?" Patch asked.

"I have loved her work when she first wrote under the pen name Flora Fairfield and then A. M. Barnard and finally under her own name." Abby pulled the magazine to her chest and exclaimed, "I just love her work."

"But it's girly." Peg sniffed. "So let's move on, please. Next."

"Okay." Abby put the magazine down and picked up a book from her lap. She opened it to the back section and read aloud, "Louisa

May Alcott was born in Germantown, Pennsylvania, in 1832. She is a best-selling novelist who has turned out a steady stream of novels and short stories, mostly for young people, drawing directly from her own family life. Her *Little Women* is considered a classic." Abby stopped and smiled at Patch. "She was a good poet, too." She thumbed through the book and stopped in the middle. "Listen to this one." She cleared her throat and read aloud, "The 'Fairy Song 'by Louisa May Alcott, 'The moonlight fades from flower and rose / And the stars dim one by one; / The tale is told, the song is sung, / And the Fairy feast is done. / The night-wind rocks the sleeping flowers, / And sings to them, soft and low. / The early birds erelong will wake: / 'T is time for the Elves to go.'

'O'er the sleeping earth we silently pass, / Unseen by mortal eye, / And send sweet dreams, as we lightly float / Through the quiet moonlit sky;-- / For the stars' soft eyes alone may see, / And the flowers alone may know, / The feasts we hold, the tales we tell; / So't is time for the Elves to go.'"

Just then, a black orderly leaned her head around the tent door and cleared her throat, "Miss Abby, your momma is wait'n for you, girl."

As Abby scooped up her books and magazine, she leaned down and kissed Patch on the cheek. "Patch, it is always such a pleasure communing with a kindred spirit. And I love you, too, Peg." Abby blew Peg a quick air kiss, spun around, gently patted Hunter on the forehead and joined the orderly as they both disappeared out the tent door, humming a gospel song together.

"Oh great," Peg huffed. "You get a kiss on the cheek, and I get an air kiss."

"Stop it. She was in a hurry."

"Stop it. She was in a hurry," Peg mocked Patch as he spit a stream of brown juice into the brass spittoon and wiped his mouth with the sleeve of his shirt.

"That nastiness there could be one reason you got an air kiss instead of the real thing."

"What?" Peg looked at him blankly.

"Never mind," Patch said, thumbing through the newspaper. "Hum, I didn't know this, but General Price was governor of Missouri from 1853 to 1857. I guess Old Pap is getting home sick."

"Why? What makes you say that?" Peg asked absently, scooting back in his chair, still miffed about getting only an air kiss.

"It says here he has put together a band of 12,000 warriors and 16 cannons. And with Marmaduke, Shelby and Fagan, he has left Pocahontas, up in the northeastern section of Arkansas, and is headed for St. Louis, 200 miles to the north."

"Hey, some southern gentlemen still know who to take it to the enemy," Peg sniffed and pushed back confidently in his chair.

Patch avoided Peg's comments and offered instead, "General Price marched from northeast Arkansas into Missouri, then through Doniphan and Fredericktown before stopping at Pilot Knob, 80 miles shy of St. Louis. He stopped when he got news that the Yankees had puffed up their troop count in St. Louis by another 6,000 fresh and heavily armed soldiers. General Price quickly turned left instead and marched the 150 miles to the state's capital, Jefferson City. En route he burned bridges and tore up railroad tracks, while collecting 2,000 small arms and 200 wagons. He made another quick left hand turn when he found out that the capital had 12,000 Federals guarding it."

"It sounds like he is tearing up Missouri, if you ask me," Peg crowed.

Patch continued reading, "He picked up his leisure pace when he found out that 6,000 Federals had been dispatched from St.

Louis to attack his rear flank. He stopped and dug in at Boonville, 60 miles northwest of Jefferson City. He was joined by Rebel sympathizers, including guerrilla leaders 'Bloody Bill 'Anderson and George Todd. After a couple of days, he decided to leave when he got word that General Pleasonton's 8,000 men from Jefferson City had been joined with 9,000 additional Yankee infantrymen and were all headed in his direction. General Price marched toward Lexington but got headed off by 2,000 fast moving Yankee cavalry troops, so he decided to march on Independence instead. At Westport, Missouri, Price's troops got squeezed between Pleasonton's troops from his rear and Curtis' troops from his front. Wow. It says that 45,000 Northerners and Southerners collided in the largest Civil War battle fought west of the Mississippi River."

Peg mumbled something but was too busy to say anything more. He had stuck a dirty finger into his mouth to dislodge tobacco stuck between his cheek and gums.

Patch shivered in disgust and continued, "It says as Price escaped into Kansas, he fought three running battles that all happened on the same day. The first was early in the morning at Marais des Cygnes. The next was the Battle of Mine Creek, which is also known as the Battle of the Osage. And the last battle of the day was near the Marmiton River." Patch sipped his coffee and added, "For the Rebels, Mine Creek was the worst of the three. The Yankees overtook the Confederates as they were crossing Mine Creek with 500 wagons filled with needed supplies for the Southern war effort. Slowed by the wagons crossing the ford, the Rebels formed a battle line on the north side of Mine Creek. The Federals, although outnumbered, commenced the attack."

"Outnumbered? That sounds like a dumb thing to do," Peg charged.

"Yes. You would think, but listen to this. Although the Confederates had numerical superiority, they were overwhelmed by the rapid attack and the greater Federal firepower, which included revolvers and breech-loading carbines, while the Confederates fought back with older muzzle-loading rifles."

(Dream)

General Marmaduke stepped away from his dying horse and was just about to shoot it when Hunter pulled up to a stop next to him. The general jumped up, grabbed Hunter by the front of his shirt and yanked him off his horse. He pressed him to the ground with his knee and pointed the gun in his face and hissed, "Are you a Yankee or a Rebel?"

Hunter, spitting dust and dirt out of his mouth, tried to answer, "I'm. I'm. I'm." Hunter, blinking tears away, stammered in a broken voice, "Sir, I've got the measles and was kicked in the head by a mule."

"It doesn't matter what you are," the general said as he pushed Hunter back down to the ground. The general smiled, "I'm going to take your horse anyway, Mister Measles."

"And Mister General, I think I'm going to take you as my prisoner," a voice behind the general said as it pressed the barrows of its shotgun between the general's shoulder blades.

General Marmaduke spun around angrily and slapped the shotgun aside, "You can't capture me, private." He huffed. "Can't you see I'm a general?"

The Yankee private stepped a few steps back and raised his shotgun toward the general's chest, "I'm sorry, sir. My Old Miss Mary Todd here, she don't know the difference between a general and private."

(Hospital)

"Read that again," Peg insisted.

"It says that mass confusion reigned on the Mine Creek

battlefield as many of Price's men had donned captured Union uniforms, making it harder to distinguish between them and real Federal soldiers. General Marmaduke was captured by an Iowa trooper named James Dunlavy, as he went to rally what he thought was a group of his own men, but who turned out to belong to Benteen's command. General Cabell similarly became a prisoner, as would nearly 1,000 of Price's army by the time the battle ended. What was left of Price's army fled from Kansas and headed south into the safety of the friendly Indian Territory, thus sealing its fate and ending his disastrous Missouri Expedition."

"Ah, my main man Marmaduke? Captured?" Peg whined.

Patch read quietly for a moment then added, "On his march back to Arkansas, Price had to avoid the Union troops at Fort Smith, so he took a wide arch south through Indian Territory and finally reentered Arkansas at the busy little Red River town of Laynesport (near Ashdown). Even though he returned with only one third of the men he left with, he happily reported to his superiors that his campaign had hopefully prevented Abraham Lincoln from getting reelected. And that, in three short months, he had marched 1,434 miles, fought 43 battles and skirmishes, captured and paroled over 3,000 Federal officers and men, captured 18 pieces of artillery and destroyed Missouri railroad tracks, bridges and property valued at over $10,000,000."

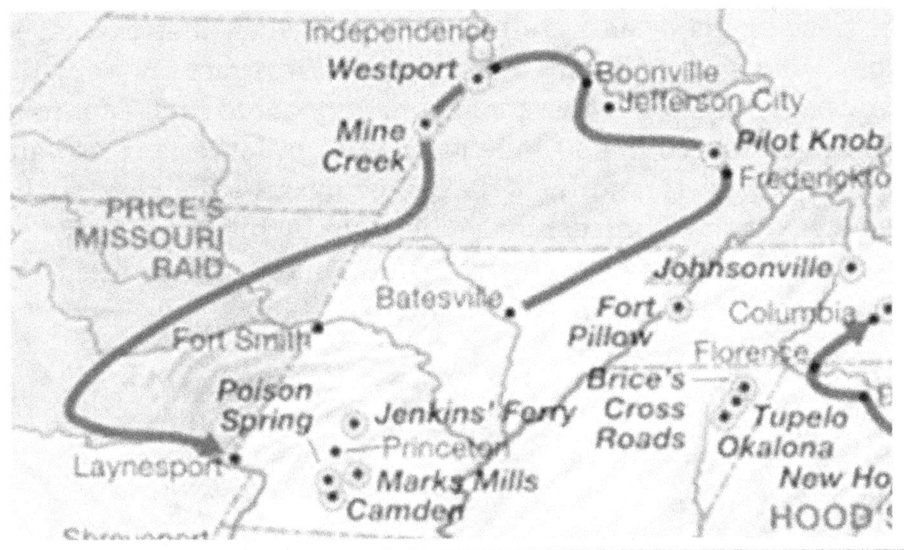

"All I can say is 'The PRICE is right!'" Peg hooted.

"Right or wrong, General Price returned to a mess. When he took 12,000 troops and left on his Missouri expedition, he left a void that was quickly filled with lawless thugs who killed and plundered at will all over Arkansas. One citizen professed, 'Noncombatants were the biggest victims of the war. 'South of the Arkansas River, Bushwhackers and Partisan Rangers harassed farm families and citizens. North of the Arkansas River, farm families and citizens were harassed by Jayhawkers or by crazed and zealous abolitionists. The Yankees could offer the citizens no safety either. In fact, it says here they were thinking about abandoning Fort Smith because its supply trains kept being hit by Southern marauders. And in General Price's absence, what few troops that were left, commanded by General Magruder, were kept in the southwest corner of the state to protect Camden and Governor Flanagin at Washington, the new capital."

"That's it - thugs and marauders?" Peg lamented.

Pretty much. General Steele, who felt his job was in jeopardy because of his often miss-handling of civilian matters, called for a raid into Southern Arkansas, as a distraction from his leadership problems. He sent Major Avery out to forage for food and livestock. In his 80 mile journey from Little Rock toward Princeton, Avery and his 470 Yankee troops were continually mauled, not by Confederate soldiers but by hit-and-run armed thugs and ruffians. He was hit at Tulip, Benton and ambushed at Hurricane Creek near Benton."

Gov. Harris Flanagin Washington

Gov. Isaac Murphy
Little Rock

"Thugs and ruffians, my, my," Peg fretted.

"It says here that the citizens in the south pleaded with Governor Flanagin for help and protection. And the citizens in the north portion of the state were petrified with fear when General Steele got replaced, and they started pulling Union troops out of Fort Smith. They sent a plea to General Grant not to abandon the fort and the thousands of citizens who would be left unprotected and exposed the 'assassins and robbers.'"

"Assassins and robbers! What happened to the Gentleman's War?" Peg pondered to himself.

"It looks like the Yankees are getting ready to move the G. War. to the E.A.S.T." Patch took a sip of coffee.

"What does that mean?" Peg twisted his nose and looked perplexed at Patch.

"It says here General Ulysses S Grant started pulling Union troops out of Arkansas in huge numbers to support Sherman's march to the sea and to help crush the last remaining Confederate sea port at Mobile, Alabama. It says that the Department of Arkansas headed up by the Yankee General Reynolds had only 10,000 cavalry and 12,000 infantry to cover the whole state of Arkansas."

"I don't know where you're from, but that still sounds like a lot of dad-burn Yankees to me."

"Reynolds didn't think so. Instead of mounting any major offensives, it seems he struck a defensive posture and did what General Grant proposed – protect the citizens and dominate the waterways. He strengthened his positions at Little Rock and along a line of posts that ran from Helena to De Valls Bluff to the capital city." Patch took a sip of coffee and continued, "When citizens petitioned the Unionist governor Isaac Murphy for more and better protection, General Reynolds beefed up the troop numbers at Fort Smith and the forts at Van Buren, Clarksville and Fayetteville. It says that the Yankee's military numbers started to grow as Arkansans who supported the Union enlisted to protect their families and their state and take it back from the marauding thugs and bands of graybacks."

"Marauding thugs, Bushwhackers and bands of graybacks, my, my," Peg groaned.

"This will tickle your fancy." Patch smiled to himself and continued, "Many of the growing Union enlistments were made up of freed slaves from Arkansas and Mississippi plantations."

"What? No Indians?" Peg spit a stream of brown juice into the brass spittoon and wiped his mouth with the sleeve of his shirt.

CHAPTER 15 - DARDANELLE, IVEY'S FORD, APPOMATTOX & MEXICO

(Hospital)

Patch sat quietly thumbing through the newspaper. "This is interesting," Patch said, folding the newspaper back. "It looks like not everything is Bushwhackers and Jayhawkers. It says here that 1,500 Rebel soldiers from Brooks and Newton regiments and Captain Stirman's brigade have set up an ingenious trap near Dardanelle at Ivey's Ford. It says that steamboats coming from Fort Smith down the Arkansas River have to come around a blind and narrow bend in the river at Ivey's Ford and are on top of the Rebel's artillery before they can stop and try to back up, since there is no room to turn around."

(Dream)

Hunter watched as the New Chippewa steamed quickly around the blind bend. As it did, it was immediately raked with artillery and rifle fire. In minutes, it ran aground and lay beached, helpless to the marauders that swarmed over it like ants. Hunter and his horse dutifully followed Colonel Brooks to the side of the boat. "Sergeant Major," Colonel Brooks bellowed, "What do we have?" The Colonel turned to Hunter and ordered, "Write this report down, boy."

The Sergeant Major briefly checked his notepad and hollered from the pilot's house, "We captured thirty men of the Fiftieth Indiana Infantry Regiment, forty freedmen, the vessel's captain and crew and several Unionist refugee families."

"Hunter, go help the Sergeant Major set the steamer on fire."

"Sir, I've got the measles and was kicked in the head by a mule," *Hunter whined.*

"Shut up and go do as I ordered." With that, Colonel Brooks pushed Hunter off his horse with the tip of his sword.

As Hunter helped the Rebels put the torch to the New Chippewa, the Annie Jacobs steamed into sight around the blind bend. Her captain must have spotted the stricken New Chippewa, but instead of stopping and trying to back up, decided to try and run past the Rebel guns. The Rebel artillery piece was ready and hammered the steamer mercilessly. Soon, she too ran aground on the north bank of the river after being hit at least fifteen times. Within minutes, another paddle-wheeler, the Lotus, steamed into range of the Confederate cannon and was hit five times before running aground on the north bank near the Annie Jacobs.

The Sergeant Major grabbed Hunter and spun him around. "Go help with the cannon," the Sergeant Major ordered, pushing Hunter in that direction. "The axle is broken, and we have to get it out of here quick before the place starts swarming with even more Yankees."

(Hospital)

"Read that again," Peg insisted

"The Yankee commander gathered the Union troops from the beached Annie Jacobs and the Lotus and sent word to a nearby forage train guarded by more than 100 Kansas cavalrymen to come to the aid of the stricken vessels. He also sent messengers to the Admiral Hines to keep her from steaming into the Confederate's trap and to Fort Smith for reinforcements." Patch sipped his coffee and added, "The Rebel's artillery piece was disabled with a broken axle, and seeing the approaching cavalry reinforcements, the Confederates broke off their very successful river engagement and headed south 80 miles to Caddo Gap. Later, they pulled back to the safety of southwestern Arkansas.

And for the next few months, until the end of the war, their fight plan was one of defense and not attack. General Magruder had his troops defending Washington and the manufacturing capabilities that had been constructed at Camden, Lewisville and Falcon."

"End of the war?" Peg scrunched up his face and fish-eyed Patch sideways.

Surrender At Appomattox

(Dream)

Everyone watched, as General Grant took longer than necessary to light his cigar. He puffed on it and blew a white puffy cloud toward Hunter. "Read the surrender document," he ordered. "And have these gentlemen sign it when you are through."

Hunter cleared his throat nervously. "We, the undersigned Prisoners of War, belonging to the Army of Northern Virginia, having been this day surrendered by General Robert E. Lee, C.S.A., Commanding said Army to Lieutenant General U. S. Grant, Commanding Armies of United States, do hereby give our solemn parole of honor that we will not hereafter serve in the armies of the Confederate States or in any military capacity whatever, against the United States of America or under aid to the enemies of the latter, until properly exchanged in such manner as shall be mutually approved by the respective authorities. Done at Appomattox Court House, Va. this 9th day of April, 1865. R. E. Lee, General W. H. Taylor, Lt. Colonel Charles S. Venaber, Lt. Col. adjutant Charles Marshal, Lt. Col. & Inspector General W. E. Pentin, Lt. Col. Gilbert B. Cooke, Major H. S. Young, Major The within named men will not be disturbed by United States authorities, so long as they observe their parole and the laws in force where they may reside."

(Hospital)

"Don't bother to read that again." Peg spit a stream of brown juice into the brass spittoon and wiped his mouth with the sleeve of his shirt and added, "So much for the war east of the Mississippi River, but how about our boys out here west of the Mississippi River?"

"It says here, 'That though Confederate forces west of the Mississippi River, in the Trans-Mississippi Theater, did not officially surrender until June 2, 1865, a significant portion of Confederate forces in Arkansas already surrendered or disbanded. The majority of Arkansas 'active soldiers 6,000 surrendered at Jacksonport along with Brigadier General M. Jeff Thompson, 'The Swamp Fox, 'on May 11, 1865.'" Patch paused then added, "This is interesting. The very next day at Palmito Ranch the 'last battle 'of the Civil War west of the Mississippi took place. Some 250 men of the 62nd U.S. Colored Infantry Regiment and 50 men of the 2nd Texas Cavalry Regiment under the command of a Yankee colonel named Barrett jumped our boys down near where the Rio Grande in Texas empties into the Gulf of Mexico. They fought for two days until our boys under the command of "Rip" Ford drove the Yankees off. And that was it. Other than a small military engagement near the end of the month at Monticello, Arkansas, that was the end to the end."

"Wow. April 9ᵗʰ until June 2nd, I guess bad news travels slowly." Peg rubbed his beard furiously in disbelief and added a question. "And the war really is over?"

"Yes, for most but not the Indians. It says here that General Stand Watie finally put down his guns and surrendered to the Union troops only after he got the news that President Jefferson Davis was captured at Irwinville, Georgia on May 10th. Chief Watie surrendered the last organized Confederate military force at Doaksville in Indian Territory, June 23rd, 1865, over 60 days after Appomattox."

"I guess that is the end of the Confederate States of America," Peg said reflectively.

"Not yet. Many Confederate officers and soldiers took off for Mexico to regroup and to keep the Confederate States of America alive so that someday they could fight again."

"True Confederate gentlemen," Peg said, pushing himself confidently back into his chair and adjusting his hat. "Who went?"

"Well, you'll recognize this general's name, John Magruder. After the Ivey's Ford attacks on the Arkansas River, he returned to southwest Arkansas to defend the manufacturing capabilities that had been constructed in and around Camden."

"Our General Sterling Price went too. Remember only six months before the war ended he took 12,000 warriors and 16 cannons into Missouri on his 'Great Raid 'to capture St. Louis? Or how about Thomas Hindman, your old buddy. Remember he gave us the Partisan Rangers who quickly turned into 'Bushwhackers'? Well, he scurried off to Mexico with his family."

"Hindman? Oh, yeah, the T-zar of Little Rock." Peg snorted.

Patch sipped his coffee and continued. "How about General Cadmus Wilcox, also known as 'Billy Fixin'? He fought at the Battle of Seven Pines, at Battle of Fredericksburg, at the Battle of Chancellorsville and at the Battle of Gettysburg. This guy was not about to give up and go home. He still had more war to fight."

"So they all went to Mexico?" Peg muttered quizzically.

"Yep. In fact General Jo Shelby led a whole brigade of unrepentant Confederates into exile across the Rio Grande at Eagle Pass on July 4th, 1865. Some Confederates who fled to Mexico were facing federal indictments for treason. However, many left because they despised the idea of living under their Federal conquerors. The pro-Confederate Mexican Emperor Maximilian welcomed the Rebels and gave them free land to colonize. 'Carlota,' named after his wife, was the most notable colony." Patch turned the page and continued, "However, within five years, all of the colonies failed to flourish, and returning ex-confederates, under blanket amnesties from the U.S. Government, were strangers in a strange land. But they all went on to lend their energies and enterprise to the rebuilding of the South, finally closing the last chapter of the Civil War."

Abraham Lincoln
16th President

John Wilkes Booth
Assassin

Peg cleared his throat. "It's sad that President Lincoln got assassinated six days after the surrender at Appomattox." He paused and then offered thoughtfully. "You know, there wasn't a day of his four years in office that the country wasn't torn apart and at war. All I can say is may the poor man rest in peace, finally."

"I guess war does not determine who is right — only who is left," Patch said as he folded the newspaper closed.

The End

ABOUT THE AUTHOR

Juian Olson

Jinx (Julian) Olson was born on July 18th, 1940 in the small farming town of Swifton, located in the northeastern part of Arkansas (west of Jonesboro). He was raised in Taylor Township near Detroit Michigan, but spent many of his long and lazy summer vacations on his grandfather Otto Julian's farm. His mother's maiden name was Thompson.

At seventeen he joined the Navy and went to California. After four years in the Navy, on an aircraft carrier and in San Diego, he spent the next forty years living, working and raising a family of two girls in Northern California, San Francisco Bay Area and Silicon Valley. After getting his MBA degree and while working on his Doctorate in Business Administration, he spent a long and successful career in the computer and high-tech industry in sales, marketing, public relations and advertising. After his sad divorce of thirty-six years, he retired and moved back to his Southern roots in Swifton. In addition to a new career in writing books, he has joined the Gideons International to help pass out Bibles in hotel, motel and hospital rooms across America and the main stream of life.

Other books by the author (available at Amazon.com):

-Disposable Human Beings - Kiwi Cay (An apocalyptic view of technology and the future of mankind)
-Hunter Jones Joins the Civil War... (Missouri)
-Hunter Jones Joins the Civil War... (Indian Territory)
-Hunter Jones Joins the Civil War... (Arkansas)
-Soul Mate Left Behind (A marriage self-help book)